γ P.T.

This man was of a medical tea

To save lives and then use his medical knowledge to declare this island unfit for human habitation. The tough decisions would be made and he'd move on to the next crisis. To the next need.

But for now that need was hers. She clung and took her strength here, where it was offered. She melted into him for this one harsh kiss, this kiss that must end.

They knew it.

It tore Morag apart. It seemed that in this overwhelming chaos all she had between her and madness was the touch of Grady's mouth.

He'd stay with her whatever it took, the kiss said, but she knew it wasn't true.

He'd stay with her only until tomorrow.

Marion Lennox was born on an Australian dairy farm.
She moved on—mostly because the cows weren't
interested in her stories! Marion writes Medical
Romance™ as well as Tender Romance™. Initially she
used different names, so if you're looking for past
books, search also for author Trisha David. In her non-
writing life Marion cares (haphazardly) for her
husband, teenagers, dogs, cats, chickens and anyone
else who lines up at her dinner table. She fights her
rampant garden (she's losing) and her house dust
(she's lost). She also travels, which she finds seriously
addictive. As a teenager Marion was told she'd never
get anywhere reading romance. Now romance is the
basis of her stories, her stories allow her to travel, and
if ever there was an advertisement for following your
dream, she'd be it! Marion Lennox is an award-
winning author. You can contact Marion at
www.marionlennox.com

THE DOCTOR'S RESCUE MISSION

BY
MARION LENNOX

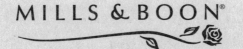

MILLS & BOON®

For Mum, who likes her romances dangerous.
With love.

First published in Great Britain 2005
Harlequin Mills & Boon Limited,
Eton House, 18-24 Paradise Road, Richmond, Surrey TW9 1SR

© Marion Lennox 2005

ISBN 0 263 84297 5

Set in Times Roman 10 on 11¼ pt.
03-0405-52185

Printed and bound in Spain
by Litografia Rosés, S.A., Barcelona

CHAPTER ONE

THE call came as Morag prepared for dinner with the man she intended to share her life with. By the time he arrived, Dr Grady Reece was thrust right out of the picture.

The moment she opened the door, Grady guessed something was wrong. This man's career involved responding to disaster, and disaster was etched unmistakably on her face.

'What is it, Morag?'

That was almost her undoing. The way he said her name. She'd always disliked her name. It seemed harsh—a name suggestive of rough country, high crags and bleak weather—but the lilt in Grady's voice the first time he'd uttered it had made her think it was fine after all.

'We need to talk,' she managed. 'But…your family is expecting us.' Grady's brother was a prominent politician and they'd been invited to a family barbecue at his huge mansion on North Shore.

'Rod won't miss us,' Grady told her. 'You know I'm never tied down. My family expect me when they see me.'

That was the way he wanted it. She'd learned that about him early, and she not only expected it but she liked it. Loose ties, no clinging—it was the way to build a lasting relationship.

No ties? What was she about to do?

Dear heaven.

'You want to tell me now?' he asked, and she shook her head. She needed more time. A little more time. Just a few short minutes of the life she'd so carefully built.

'Hey.' He touched her face and smiled down into her eyes. 'I'll take you somewhere I know,' he told her. 'And don't look like that. Nothing's so bad that we can't face it together.'

Together…

There was to be no more together. She fought for control as she grabbed her coat. *Together*.

Not any more.

He didn't press her. He led her to the car and helped her in, knowing instinctively that she was fighting to maintain control.

He was so good in a crisis.

Grady was three years older than Morag, and he'd qualified young from medical school. He had years more experience than she did in dealing with crises.

His reaction to disaster was one of the things that had drawn her to him, she thought as she stared despairingly across the car at the man she loved—and wondered how she could bear to tell him what she must.

Patients talked to him when they were in trouble, she thought. So must she.

Grady was a trauma specialist with Air-Sea Rescue, a team that evacuated disaster victims from all over Australia. Wherever there was disaster, there was Grady, and he was one of the best.

He'd arrive in the emergency room with yet another appallingly injured patient, and the place would be calmer for his presence. Tall and muscular, with a shock of curly black hair and deep, brown, weather-crinkled eyes, Grady's presence seemed to radiate a reassurance that was as inexplicable as it was real. Trust me, those crinkling eyes said. You'll be OK with me.

And why wouldn't you trust him? The man was heart-warmingly gorgeous. Morag hadn't been able to believe her luck when he'd asked her out.

As a surgical registrar, Morag's job at Sydney Central included assessing patients pre-surgery. She'd first met Grady as he'd handed over a burns victim—an aging hippie who'd gone to sleep still smoking his joint. The man's burns had been appalling.

Morag had been impressed with Grady's concern then, and she'd been even more impressed when he'd appeared in the ward two weeks later—to drop in and say hello to someone no one in the world seemed to care about.

That had been the beginning. So far they'd only had four weeks of interrupted courtship, but she'd known from the start that this could work. They had so much in common.

They were both ambitious. They both loved working in critical care, and they intended to work in the fast lane for their entire medical careers. They laughed at the same things. They loved the same food, the same lifestyle, the same…everything.

And Grady had the ability to curl her toes. Just as he was doing now. She looked across at her with that quizzical half-smile she was beginning to love, and her heart did a crazy back somersault with pike. He looked gorgeous in his soft, lambswool sweater—a sweater that on anyone else but Grady might look effeminate, but on Grady it just looked fabulous—and it was all she could do not to burst into tears.

She didn't. Of course she didn't. Tears would achieve nothing. She turned away and stared straight ahead, into the darkness.

The restaurant he drove her to was a secluded little bistro where the food was great and the service better. Grady ordered, still sensing that Morag couldn't do anything other than focus on the catastrophe surrounding her. With wine poured and orders taken, the waiters let them be.

They must look a really romantic couple, Morag thought dully. She'd taken such care with her appearance tonight. Although dressed for a barbecue, there was little casual about her appearance. Her jeans were figure-hugging and brand-new. She wore great little designer shoes, high as high, stretching her legs to sexy-long. Her crop top was tiny, crimson, leaving little to the imagination, and she'd swept up her chestnut curls into a knot of wispy curls on top of her head. She'd applied make-up to her pale skin with care. She knew she looked sexy and seductive and expensive—and she knew that there was good reason why every man present had turned his head as Grady had ushered her into the restaurant.

This was how she loved to look. But after tonight there'd never be any call for her to look like this again.

'Hey, it can't be that bad.' Grady reached out and took her hand. He stroked the back of it with care. It was something she'd seen him do with patients.

Two weeks ago a small boy had come into Sydney Central after a tractor accident and Grady had sat with the parents and explained there was no way the little boy's arm could be saved. She'd seen him lift the burly farmer's hand and touch it just like this—an almost unheard-of gesture man to man, but so necessary when the father would be facing self-blame all his life.

She'd loved that gesture when she'd seen it then. And now, here he was, using the same gesture on her.

'What is it, Morag?'

'My sister.' She could hardly say it.

Don't say it at all! a little voice inside her head was screaming at her. If you don't say it out loud, then it won't be real.

But it was real. Horribly real.

'I didn't know you had a sister.' Grady was frowning, and Morag knew he was thinking of her mother, the brisk businesswoman to whom he'd been introduced.

'Beth's my half-sister,' Morag whispered. 'She's ten years older than I am. She lives on Petrel Island.'

'Petrel Island?'

'Off the coast of—'

'I know Petrel Island.' He was focused on her face, and his fingers were still doing the smoothing thing to the back of her hand. It was making her cringe inside. This man—he was who she wanted for ever. She knew that. But he—

'We evacuated a kid from Petrel Island twelve months back,' Grady said. 'It's a weird little community—Kooris and fishermen and a crazy doctor-cum-lighthouse-keeper keeping the whole community together.'

'That's Beth.'

'That's your sister?' His tone was incredulous and she knew

why. There seemed no possible connection between the placid islander Beth and the sophisticated career doctor he was looking at.

But there was. Of course there was. You couldn't remove sisterhood by distance or by lifestyle.

Beth was her sister for ever.

'Beth's the island doctor,' she told him, finding the courage to meet his eyes. 'She's also the lighthouse caretaker. It's what our father did so she's taken right over.'

'Beth's the lighthouse-keeper? And the doctor as well?'

'Yes.'

'But…why?'

'It's a family thing,' she told him. Seeing his confusion deepen, she tried to explain. 'Dad was born on the island, and inherited the lighthouse-keeping from my grandad. He married an island girl and they had Beth. Then the lighthouse was upgraded to automatic—just as Dad's first wife died. She was seven months pregnant with their second baby, but she collapsed and died of eclampsia before Dad could get her to the mainland.'

Grady was frowning, taking it on board with deep concern. 'She had no warning?'

'There was no doctor on the island,' Morag said bleakly. 'And, no, he had no warning. Everything seemed normal. She was planning on leaving for the mainland at thirty-four weeks but she didn't make it. Anyway, her death meant that within a few weeks Dad lost his wife, his baby son and his job. All he had left was two-year-old Beth. But the waste of the deaths made him decide what to do. He brought Beth to the mainland, and managed to get a grant to go to medical school. That's where he met my mother. They married and had me, but the marriage was a disaster. Everyone was miserable. By the time Dad finished med school, the government decided that leaving the lighthouse to look after itself—even if it was automatic— was also a disaster. The island was still desperate for a doctor, and the caretaker's cottage was still empty. So Dad and Beth went home.'

Grady's face was thoughtful. 'Leaving you behind with your mother?'

'Of course.' She shrugged. 'Can you see my mother living on Petrel Island? But I did spend lots of time there. Every holiday. Whenever I could. Mum didn't mind. As long as she wasn't seen as a deserting mother, anything I did was OK by her. She's not exactly a warm and fuzzy parent, my mother.'

'I have met her.'

He had. They'd moved fast in four weeks. Morag's eyes flickered again to his face. Maybe this could work. Maybe he…

But the eyes he was looking at her with were wrong, she thought, confused by the messages she was receiving. He was concerned as he'd be concerned for a patient. He was using a 'Let's get to the bottom of this' kind of voice. He was gentleness personified, but his gentleness was abstract. For Morag, who'd had a childhood of abstract affection, the concept was frightening.

'So you spent holidays with your father and Beth,' Grady was saying, and she forced herself to focus on the past rather than the terrifying future.

'Yes. They were… They loved me. Beth was everything to me.'

'Where's your father now?'

'He died three years ago. He's buried on the island. That's OK. He had a subarachnoid haemorrhage and died in his sleep, and it wasn't a bad way to go for a man in his seventies.'

'But Beth?'

'As I said, she's a doctor, like me.' Still she couldn't say what was wrong. How could she? How could she voice the unimaginable? 'My dad, and then Beth after him, provided the island's medical care. Because there's only about five hundred people living on the island, and the medical work is hardly arduous, they've kept on the lighthouse. too. Lighthouse-keeping's not the time consuming job it was.'

'I guess it's not.' Grady was watching her face. Waiting. Knowing that she was taking her time to say what had to be said, and knowing she needed that time. He lifted her hand again and gripped her fingers, looking down at them as if he was examining them for damage. It was a technical manoeuvre, she thought dully. Something he'd learned to do. 'So Beth's the island doctor…'

'She's great.' She was talking too fast, she thought, but she couldn't slow down. Her voice didn't seem to belong to her. 'She's ten years older than me, and she was almost a mother to me. She'd turn up unexpectedly whenever I most needed her. If I was in a school play and my mother couldn't make it—which she nearly always couldn't—I'd suddenly, miraculously, find Beth in the audience, cheering me on with an enthusiasm that was almost embarrassing. And when she decided to be a doctor, I thought I could be, too.'

'But not like Beth?'

'Beth wanted to go back to the island. It tore her apart to leave to do her medical training, and the moment she was qualified she returned. She fell in love with a local fisherman and the island's her home. She loves it.'

'And you?' he probed.

'The island's never been my home. I love it but I never thought of living anywhere but here.' She attempted a smile but it was a pretty shaky one. 'I guess I have more than a bit of my mother in me somewhere. I like excitement, cities, shopping…life.'

'Like me.'

'My excitement levels don't match your excitement levels,' she told him ruefully. 'I like being a surgeon in a bustling city hospital. I don't dangle out of helicopters in raging seas, plucking—'

But Grady wasn't to be distracted. The background had been covered. Now it was time to move on. 'Morag, what's wrong?' His deep voice cut through her misery, compelling. Doctor asking for facts, so he could treat what needed to be treated.

Her voice faltered. She looked up at him and then away. His hand tightened on hers—just as she'd seen him do with distressed patients. For some reason the action had her tugging away from him. She didn't want this man treating her as he'd treat a patient. This was supposed to be special.

This was supposed to be for ever.

For ever?

The prospect of for ever rose up, overwhelming her with dread. Somehow she had to explain and she had to do it before she broke down.

'Beth has renal cancer,' she whispered.

She'd shifted her hand back to her side of the table. Grady made a move to regain it, but she tucked it carefully under the table. It seemed stupidly important that she knew where her hand was.

He didn't say anything. She swallowed while he waited for her to go on. He was good, this man. His bedside manner was impeccable.

And suddenly, inexplicably, his bedside manner made her want to hit him.

Crazy. Anger—anger at Grady—was crazy. She had to force herself to be logical here. To make sense.

'I haven't been back to the island for over a year,' she managed. 'But last time I went Beth seemed terrific. She had a bad time for a while. She married a local fisherman, and he was drowned just after Dad died. But she was recovering. She's thirty-nine years old and she has a little boy, Robbie, who's five. She seemed settled and happy. Life was looking good.'

'But now she's been diagnosed with renal cancer?' His tone was carefully neutral, still extracting facts.

'Mmm.'

'What stage?'

'Advanced. Apparently she flew down to Melbourne last month and had scans without telling anyone. There's a massive tumour in the left kidney, with spread that's clear from the scans. It's totally inoperable.'

And totally anything else, she thought bleakly as she waited for Grady to absorb what she'd told him. He'd know the inevitable outcome just as clearly as she did. If renal cancer was caught while the tumour was still contained, then it could be surgically removed—removing the entire kidney—but once it had spread outside the kidney wall, chemotherapy or radiotherapy would make little difference.

'She's dying,' she whispered.

'I'm sorry.'

Her eyes flew up to his. He was watching her, his eyes gentle, but she wasn't imagining it. There was that tiny trace of removal. Distancing.

'I need to go to the island,' she told him. 'Now.'

'Of course you do.' He hesitated, and she could see him juggling appointments in his head. Thinking ahead to his frantic week. It was what she always did when something unexpected came up.

Until now.

'Do you want me to come with you?' he asked.

Did she? Of course she did. More than anything else in the world. But…

'I can call on Steve to cover for me for the next week,' he told her. 'If we could be back by next Sunday—'

'No.'

His face stilled. 'Sorry?'

And now it was time to say it. It couldn't be put off one moment longer.

'Grady, this isn't going to happen,' she said gently, as if this would hurt him as much as it hurt her. And maybe it would.

'My sister's dying. She has a little boy and she's a single mother. She has a community who depend on her.'

His face was almost expressionless. 'What are you saying?'

'That it'll be a lot…a lot longer than a week.'

'Can you take more than a week off?' His face changed back to the concerned, involved expression that was somehow turning her away from him. It was making her cringe inside. It was his doctor's face.

'I guess you must,' he said, thinking it through as he spoke. 'The hospital will organise compassionate leave for you for a few weeks.' He hesitated. 'I'll come for a week now, and then again for—'

'The funeral?' she finished for him, and watched him flinch. 'Morag…'

She shook her head. 'It's not going to happen.'

'I'm sorry. I shouldn't have said—'

'Oh, the funeral's going to happen,' she said, her anger directed squarely now against the appalling waste of cancer. 'Inevitably it'll happen. But as for taking compassionate leave…I can't.'

He frowned, confused. 'So you'll come back in a week or so?'

'I didn't say that.' She lifted her hands back onto the table and stared down at her fingers, as if she couldn't believe she was about to make the commitment that in truth she'd made the moment she'd heard her sister whisper, 'Renal cancer.' It was done. It was over. 'I'm not taking compassionate leave,' she said bluntly. 'I'm going to the island for ever.'

It shocked him. It shocked him right out of compassionate doctor, caring lover mode. All the things he was most good at. His brow snapped down in surprise, and his deep, dark eyes went still.

'You can't just quit.' Grady's job was his life, Morag thought hopelessly, and she could understand it. Until an hour ago she'd felt the same way. But she had no choice.

'Why can't I quit?' And then, despairingly, she added, 'How can I not?'

'Surely your sister wouldn't expect you to.'

'Beth expects nothing,' she said fiercely. 'She never has. She gives and she gives and she gives.' Their meal arrived at that moment and she stared down at it as if she didn't recognise it. Grady leaned across to place her knife and fork in her hands—

back to being the caring doctor—but she didn't even notice. 'Petrel Island needs her so much,' she whispered.

'She's their only doctor?'

'My father and then Beth,' she told him. She stopped for a minute then, ostensibly to eat but really to gather her thoughts to continue. 'Because my father was a doctor, more young families have come to the island, and the community's grown. There's fishing and kelp farming and a great little specialist dairy. But without a doctor, the Petrel Island community will disintegrate.'

'They could get someone else.'

'Oh, sure.' It was almost a jeer. 'A doctor who wants to practise in such a place? I don't think so. After…after Beth dies, maybe…I'll try to find someone, but it's so unlikely. And Beth needs my promise—that the island can continue without her.

'So you see,' she told him, cutting her steak into tiny pieces that she had no intention of eating. It was so important to concentrate. It was important to concentrate on anything but Grady. 'You see why I need to leave?'

There was a reason she couldn't look at him. She knew what his reaction would be. And here it came.

'But…you're saying this might be for ever?' He sounded appalled. As well he might.

'I'm saying for as long as I'm needed. Do I have a choice?'

He had the answer to that one. 'Yes,' he said flatly. 'Bring your sister here. You can't tell me there aren't far better medical facilities in Sydney than on Petrel Island. And who's going to be treating physician? You? You know that's a recipe for disaster. Caring for your own family… I don't think so.'

'There's no one else.'

'There's no one else in Sydney?' he asked incredulously.

'No. On the island. Beth won't leave the island.'

'She doesn't have a choice,' Grady said, the gentleness returning to his voice. Gentle but right. Sympathetic but firm. 'You have a life, Morag, and your life is here.'

'And Robbie? Her little boy? What of his life?'

'Maybe he's going to have to move on. Plenty of kids have a city life. It won't hurt him to spend a couple of months in Sydney.'

'You mean I should bring them both here while Beth dies.'

'You have a life, too,' he told her. 'It sounds dreadful—I know it does—but if your sister is dying then you have to think past the event.'

'Take care of the living?'

'That's right,' he said, his face clearing a little. 'Your sister will see that. She sounds a pragmatic person. Not selfish…'

'No. Not selfish. Never selfish.'

'You need to think long term. She'll be thinking long term.'

'She is,' Morag said dully. 'That's why she rang me. She's been ill for months and she's been searching for some way not to ask me. But it's come to this. She doesn't have a choice and neither do I. Without Beth the community doesn't have a doctor. Robbie doesn't have a mother. And I'm it.'

Silence. Then… 'Your mother?'

'You've met my mother. Barbara take care of Robbie? He's not even her grandchild. Don't be stupid.'

He looked flatly at her, aghast. 'You're not seriously suggesting you throw everything up here?' he demanded. 'Take over the care of a dying sister? Take on the mothering of a child, and the medical needs of a tiny island hundreds of miles from the mainland? Morag, you have to be kidding!'

'Do you think I'd joke about something like this?'

'Look, don't make any decisions,' he said urgently. 'Not yet. Get compassionate leave for a week or two and take it from there. I'll come over and do some reorganisation—'

'Some reorganisation?'

'I'll talk to the flying doctor service. We'll see if we can get a clinic over there once a month or so to keep the locals happy. I can organise an apartment here that'd accommodate your sister. Maybe we can figure out a long-term carer for the kid on the island. He can go to day care here while his mum's alive, and then we'll find someone to take him over long term.'

Great. For the first time since Beth had telephoned, Morag felt an emotion that was so fierce it overrode her complete and utter devastation. She raised her face to his and met his look head on. He was doing what he was so good at. Crisis management. He was taking disaster and hauling it into manageable bits.

But this was Beth. Beth!

'Do you know what love is?' she whispered.

He looked confused. 'Sure I do, Morag.' He reached forward and would have taken her hand again but she snatched it back like he'd burn her. 'You and I—'

'You and I don't have a thing. Not any more. This is Beth we're talking about. Beth. My darling sister. The woman who cares for me and loves me and who put her own life on hold for me so many times I can't think about it. You'd have me repay that by taking a couple of weeks' leave?'

'Morag, this is your life.'

'Our lives. Mine and Beth's. They intertwine. As ours— yours and mine—don't any more.' She rose and stood, staring down at him, her sudden surge of anger replaced by unutterable sadness. Unutterable weariness. 'Grady, I can't stay here,' she whispered. 'I'm going home. I'm going back to Petrel Island and I won't be coming back.'

He stayed seated, emphasising the growing gulf between them. 'But you don't want—'

'What I want doesn't come into it.'

'And what I want?'

'What's that supposed to mean?'

'I want you, Morag.'

'No.' She shook her head. 'No, you don't. You want the part of me that I thought I could become. That I thought I was. Independent career doctor, city girl, partner while we had the best fun…'

He rose then but it was different. He put his hands on her

shoulders and bent to kiss her lightly on the lips. It was a fleeting gesture but she knew exactly what he was doing, and the pain was building past the point where she could bear it. 'We did have fun,' he told her.

'We did.' She swallowed. It wasn't Grady's fault that she'd fallen hopelessly in love with him, she realised. Beth's illness wasn't his fault, and it wasn't his fault that their lives from now on would be totally incompatible.

It wasn't his fault that now he was letting her go.

For richer and for poorer. In sickness and in health. Whither thou goest, I will go…

Ha! It was never going to work. Beth needed her.

And Grady wasn't going to follow.

But his hand suddenly lifted to her face, as if he'd had second thoughts. He cupped her chin and forced her eyes to his. 'You can't go.' His voice was low, suddenly gruff and serious. The caring and competent young doctor had suddenly been replaced by someone who was unsure. 'Morag, these last few weeks… It's been fantastic. You know that I love you.'

Did he? Until this evening she'd thought—she'd hoped that he had. And she'd thought she loved him.

Whither thou goest, I will go.

No. It hadn't reached that stage yet. She looked into his uncertain eyes and she knew that the line hadn't been crossed. Which was just as well. It made the decision she was making now bearable. Just. Maybe.

'No,' she said softly. 'You don't love me. Not yet. But I do love Beth, and she needs me. The island needs me. It was wonderful, Grady, but I need to move on.'

Even then he could have stopped her. He could have come up with some sort of alternative. Come with her now, try the island for size, think of how it could work…

No. That was desperation talking and desperation had no foundation in solid, dreadful reality.

She didn't need to end this. It was already over.

'What can I do?' he asked, and she bit her lip.

'Nothing.' Nothing she could ever vocalise. 'Just say goodbye.'

And that was that.

She rose on tiptoe and kissed him again, hard this time, and fast, tasting him, savouring him for one last moment. One fleeting minute. And then, before he could respond, she'd straightened and backed away.

'I need to go, Grady,' she told him, trying desperately to keep the tears from her voice. 'It's been…fabulous. But I need…to follow my heart.'

CHAPTER TWO

MORAG felt the earth move while she was at Hubert Hamm's, and stupidly, after the first few frightening moments, she thought it mightn't matter.

Hubert was the oldest of the island's fisherman. His father had run sheep up on the ridge to the north of the island. That was where Hubert had been born and the tiny cottage was still much as Elsie Hamm had furnished it as a bride almost a hundred years before.

The cottage had two rooms. There was a tiny kitchen-living room where Robbie sat and fondled Hubert's old dog, and an even smaller bedroom where Hubert lay, approaching his death with stately dignity.

It'd be a while before he achieved his objective, Morag thought as she measured his blood pressure. Six months ago, Hubert had taken himself to bed, folded his hands across his chest and announced that the end was nigh. The only problem was that the neighbours kept dropping off wonderful casseroles and puddings, usually staying for a chat. His love of gossip was therefore thoroughly catered for. Hubert's bedroom window looked out over the whole island, and he was so eagle-eyed and interested that death seemed less and less enticing.

With Morag visiting every few days, his health did nothing but improve, to the extent that now Morag had no compunction in bringing Robbie with her as she took her weekly hike up the scree. There was a rough vehicle track round the back of the ridge but the scenery from the walking path was spectacular. She and Robbie enjoyed the hike, and they enjoyed Hubert.

Would that all deathbeds were this healthy, prolonged and cheerful.

'I'm worse?' Hubert asked—without much hope—and she grinned.

'Not so you'd notice. But you're certainly a week older and that has to count for something.'

'Death's coming. I can feel it,' he said in solemn tones, but a sea eagle chose that moment to glide past his window and his old eyes swung around to follow its soaring flight.

Death might be coming, but life was still looking good.

Consultation over.

'Have you finished? Is Mr Hamm OK?' Robbie looked up as she opened Hubert's bedroom door, and she smiled across at her nine-year-old nephew with affection.

'Mr Hamm's great. His blood pressure's fine. His heart rate's nice and steady. Our patient looks like living for at least another week—if not another decade. Are you ready to go home?'

'Yep.' Robbie gave Elspeth a final hug and rose, a freckled, skinny little redhead with a grin that reminded Morag achingly of Beth. 'When Mr Hamm dies, can I have Elspeth?'

Elspeth, an ancient golden retriever, pricked up her ears in hope, but back in the bedroom so did Hubert.

'She'll stay here until I'm gone,' the old man boomed.

'Of course she will,' Robbie said, with all the indignation of a nine-year-old who knew how the world worked. 'But you've put names on everything else.'

He had, too. In the last six months Hubert had catalogued his cottage. Everything had a name on now, right down to the battered teapot on the edge of the fire-stove. '*Iris Potter, niece in London*,' the sign said, and Morag hoped that Hubert's niece would be suitably grateful when the time came.

'There's no name on Elspeth,' Robbie said reasonably. 'And she's an ace dog.'

'Yeah, well, you're a good lad,' Hubert conceded from his bed. 'She'd have a good home with you.'

'I bet she could catch rabbits.'

'My oath,' Hubert told them, still from behind the bedroom door. 'You should see her go.'

'You know, you could get up and show Robbie,' Morag said, trying not to smile, and had a snort of indignation for her pains.

'What, me? A dying man? You know…'

But she never found out what she was supposed to know. Right at that moment the house gave a long, rolling shudder. The teapot, balanced precariously on the side of the stove, tipped slowly over and crashed to the floor.

For one long moment Morag didn't realise what was happening. Then she did. Unbelievably, she did. It seemed impossible but there was no time to wonder if she was right or not.

Earthquake?

'Robbie, out! Get away from the house.' She shoved Robbie out the door before he could utter a response. Elspeth gave a terrified whimper and bolted after him, and they were barely clear before Morag was back in the bedroom, hauling Hubert out of bed and of the house after Robbie and Elspeth.

'What the…?' For someone supposedly ready to meet his maker, Hubert clearly had a way to go. He was white with terror. Morag was practically carrying him across the cottage floor as his old feet tried their hardest to scuttle on a surface that was weirdly unstable.

'It must be an earthquake.' She had him clear of the doorway now. Robbie was crouched on the back lawn, holding onto Elspeth, and the dog was whimpering in terror.

'I don't believe it.' Hubert sank to his knees and grabbed his dog as well. 'We haven't had one of these on the island for eighty years.'

They were clear now of anything that could fall. The earth seemed to be steadying again and she had everyone well away from the house. Morag was hugging Robbie, and Robbie and Hubert were both hugging Elspeth, so they were crazily attached. It was a weird intimacy in the face of shared peril.

They didn't talk. Talking seemed impossible. They just knelt and waited for a catastrophe that…that suddenly seemed as if it might not happen.

More silence. It was almost eerie. They sat and waited some more but the tremors seemed to have stopped.

Then they sat up and unattached themselves. Sort of. A bit.

'Was it really an earthquake?' Robbie demanded, and when Morag nodded, he let out his breath in one long 'Cool…'

But his body was still pressed against Morag's and he was still holding on.

'We haven't had one of these for eighty years,' Hubert whispered.

'You've experienced this before?'

'We're on some sort of fault line,' Hubert told them, his colour and his bravado returning as the ground settled. 'A bunch of scientists came here years back and did some testing but no one took much notice.' He snorted, his courage building by the minute. 'It'll be the same as last time. A bit of a wobble and a fuss and then naught for another eighty years.'

'I hope you're right.' Morag grabbed Robbie around his middle and hugged, hard. Her little nephew was usually the bravest of kids but it didn't take much for him to remember that the world was inherently unsafe. His 'cool' had been decidedly shaky. Seven years ago his father had drowned, and four years back he'd lost his mother. Now he clung alternately to Morag and the dog, and Morag kissed his hair and hugged him tight and wondered where to go to from here.

The only damage up on the ridge seemed to be a dent in Hubert's teapot. But down below… She shaded her eyes, trying to see down to the little village built around the harbour. It was a gorgeous day. The sleepy fishing village was far below them, but from here it looked untouched.

Maybe a dented teapot was the worst of it.

Please…

'Maybe you'd better stay up here for a bit in case another shock comes,' Hubert told her, his voice showing that he was just as wobbly as Robbie.

But she had no choice. She was the island's only doctor and if there was trouble in the township…

'I need to head back to check the lighthouse and radio the mainland,' she told Hubert, but she was speaking to Robbie as well. There was a bit of a stacks-on-the-mill process happening here. Robbie was on her knees, Elspeth was sprawled over Robbie, and Morag had a feeling that if dignity hadn't been an issue then Hubert would be up here as well. Nothing like the earth trembling to make you unsure of your foundations.

Robbie sat even more firmly in her lap. 'I think we should all stay here,' he told her. 'What if it gets worse?'

'Aftershocks,' Hubert said wisely. He'd moved away a little in an attempt to regain his dignity. Now he clicked his fingers for Elspeth to come to him. Elspeth wriggled higher onto Robbie's lap and Hubert had to sidle closer himself to pat his dog.

They were depending on her, Morag thought despairingly. So what was new? The entire island depended on her—when often all she wanted to do was wail.

This was an earthquake. This was truly scary. Who did she get to tremble on?

No one. Ever. She swallowed and fought for calm and for sense.

'Hubert's right. Mild earth tremors are nothing to worry about.' She put Robbie gently aside and ruffled his hair. 'Robbie, you know I need to go.' She sent him a silent message with her eyes, saying she was depending on him.

And Robbie responded. He'd learned from birth what was expected of him as the doctor's kid, and he rose to the occasion now.

'Do you really have to go?' he asked.

'You know that I do.'

'Can I come with you?'

'It'd better if you stayed here for a bit.'

He took a deep breath. He really was the best kid. 'OK.' Elspeth got a hard hug. 'I'll look after Elspeth if Mr Hamm looks after me.'

'Is that OK with you, Mr Hamm?' she asked, and Hubert flashed her a worried look.

'It's fine by me, girl, but you—'

'I'll be fine.'

'You know, the first quake is usually the biggest,' Robbie volunteered. It really hadn't been a very big shake and it was already starting to recede to adventure rather than trouble. 'I read about them in my nature book. There's not likely to be another bigger one. Just little aftershocks.'

'That's a relief.'

'Maybe a bigger one'd be cool.'

'No,' Morag said definitely. 'It wouldn't be cool.'

'Or maybe this was a ginormous one out to sea and we just got the little sideways shocks a long way away,' he said, optimism returning minute by minute.

'Well, that'd be better,' Morag conceded, thinking about it. 'With the closest land mass being the mainland three hundred miles away, there's not much likelihood of any damage at all. Mind, a few dolphins might be feeling pretty seasick.'

Robbie chuckled.

And that was that.

The earthquake was over. Even Elspeth started to wag her tail again.

But she still had to check the village.

Robbie's chuckle was a good sound, Morag thought as she started down the scree. She'd worked hard on getting that sound back after his mother had died and now she treasured it. It was a major reason she was here, on this island.

Without a life.

Who was she kidding? She had a life. She had a community to care for. She had Robbie's chuckle. And she had flying teapots to check out.

But it didn't stop her mind from wandering.

Even though she lived in one of the most isolated places in the world, there was little enough time for her to be alone. She had so many demands made on her. If it wasn't her patients it was Robbie, and although she loved the little boy to bits, this time scrambling down the scree when she wasn't much worried about what she'd find below was a time to be treasured.

She liked being alone.

No, she thought. She didn't. Here she was seldom by herself, but *alone* was a concept that had little to do with people around her.

She liked being by herself for a while. But she didn't like *alone*.

Always at the back of her heart was Grady. The life she'd walked away from.

There was no turning back, but her loss of Grady was still an aching grief, shoved away and never allowed to surface. But it was always there.

He'd written her the loveliest letter when Beth had died, saying how much he missed her, offering to take her away for a holiday, offering to organise things in Sydney so she could return, offering everything but himself.

She'd taken the letter up to the top of the lighthouse. There she'd torn it into a thousand pieces and let it blow out to sea.

Enough. Enough of Grady. She hadn't heard from him for four years.

Concentrate on need.

Surely an earthquake was worth concentrating on.

Two hundred yards down the path she paused. The closer she came to the village the more it looked as if there was no damage at all.

Hubert really did treasure his isolation. The path up to his cottage was little more than a goat track on the side of a steep incline. She could stand here for a moment with the sun on her face, look out at the breathtaking beauty of the ocean beyond the island and wonder how she could ever dream of leaving such a place. It was just beautiful.

The sea wasn't where it was supposed to be.

She blinked for a moment, thinking her eyes were playing tricks. The tide's a long way out, she thought inconsequentially, and then she thought, No, it's a crazy way out. The beach was normally twenty or thirty yards wide but now…the water seemed to have been sucked…

Sucked.

A jangling, dreadful alarm sounded in her head as her eyes swept the horizon. She was suddenly frantic. Her feet were starting to move even as she searched, hoping desperately not to see…

But she saw.

There was a long line of silver, far out. She thought she was imagining it at first—thought it must be the product of dread. Maybe it was the horizon.

Only it wasn't. It was a faint line beneath the horizon, moving inexorably closer. If it hadn't been such a calm, still day she might not have seen it at all, for in deep water it was only marginally above the height of a biggish swell, but she was sure… There was a boat far out and she saw it bucket high—unbelievably high—and then disappear behind a wall of water.

No.

The villagers were out of their cottages. She could see them. They were gathering in the street beyond the harbour. They'd be comparing notes about damage from the tremor, fearing more. They wouldn't be turned toward the sea.

She was running now, racing up the goat path. She'd never moved so fast in her life.

At least she knew what needed to be done. This place had been the graveyard for scores of ships in the years since the first group of Scottish fishermen had built their homes here, and the islanders were geared for urgent warning. The track she was on overlooked the entire island. There were bells up here, set up to make the villagers aware that there was an urgent, life-threatening need. At every curve in the track—every couple of hundred yards—there was a bell, and every island child knew the way to be sent to Coventry for ever was to ring one needlessly.

Morag knew exactly where the closest one was, and her feet

had never moved so fast as they did now. Seconds after she'd first heard her own mental alarm bell, she reached the closest warning place and the sound of the huge bell rang out across the island.

This wasn't a shipwreck. It was the islanders themselves who were in deadly peril.

They'd have to guess what she was warning of. 'Guess,' she pleaded. 'Guess.'

They heard. The islanders gathered in the street stilled. She saw them turn to face her as they registered the sound of the bell.

She was too far away to signal danger. She was too far away for her scream to be heard.

But there were fishermen among the villagers, old heads whose first thoughts went to the sea. They'd see a lone figure far up on the ridge ringing the bell. Surely they'd guess.

Maybe they'd guess?

She stood on the edge of the rocky outcrop and waved her arms, pointing out to sea, screaming soundlessly into the stillness. Guess. Guess.

And someone responded. She saw rather than heard the yell erupting—a scream of warning and of terror as someone figured out what she might be warning them about. Someone had put together the tremor and her warning and they knew what might happen.

Even from so far away, she heard the collective response.

People were yelling for their children. People were grabbing people. People were running. A mass of bodies was hurling off the main street, scrabbling for the side streets that led steeply out of town.

She could see them but she could do nothing except go back to uselessly ringing her damned bell.

People were stumbling, stopping to help, to carry...

'*No*,' she was screaming, helpless in the face of the sheer distance between here and the town. '*Don't stop. Don't stop.*'

She could see their terror. She felt it with them.

And she could see the smaller and smaller distance between the islanders and the great wash of water bearing down.

'*Run. Run.*'

The wall of water was building now as it approached land. It was sucking yet more water up before it. The shore was a barren wasteland of waterless emptiness.

And Morag could do nothing. She could only stand high on the hill and watch the tsunami smash toward the destruction of her people.

There was a soft, growing rumble. Louder…

Then it hit.

She watched in appalled, stupefied fascination as the water reached the shore. There were dull grating sounds as buildings ground together. Sharp reports as power poles snapped. It was a vast front of inrushing water, smashing all before it in a ghastly, slamming tide, the like of which Morag had never begun to imagine.

And there was nothing to do where she stood but watch.

Maybe she could have closed her eyes. She surely didn't want to see, but for the first awful seconds her eyes stayed open.

She saw the tiny harbour surge, boats pushed up onto the jetty, houses hit, the water almost to their eaves. Dear God, if people were inside…

She saw old Elias Cartwright open his front door just as the water hit—stubborn old Elias who'd consider it beneath his dignity to gather outside with the villagers just because of a mere earth tremor…

The water smashed and that was the last Morag saw of Elias.

It was then that she closed her eyes and she felt herself start to retch.

She kept her eyes closed.

Closed.

This was safe. Here in the dark she could tell herself she was retching for nothing. It was a dream—a nightmare—and soon she'd wake up.

But there was no line separating dream from reality.

The sun was still warm on her face. One of the island goats was nudging her arm in gentle enquiry. The world was just the same.

Only, of course, it wasn't. When she finally found the courage to open her eyes, the tiny Petrel Island settlement was changed for ever.

The houses nearest the harbour were gone. The harbour itself was a tangle of timber and mud and uprooted trees.

Devastation…

Her first thought flew to Robbie.

She looked upward to Hubert's place and the old man was staring down at her, her horror reflected in the stock-still stance of the old man. She was two hundred yards away but his yell echoed down the scree with the clarity of a man with twenty-year-old lungs.

'I'll take care of the lad. We'll watch the sea for more. Robbie and I'll stick with the bell and not leave it.'

She managed to listen. She managed to understand what he'd said.

Hubert and Robbie would watch to warn of another wave, she thought dully. And in offering to take care of Robbie, she knew what Hubert was saying she should do.

She was the island's only doctor. The islanders looked to her for help. For leadership.

She had to go down.

CHAPTER THREE

'NOTHING ever happens in this place.'

Dr Grady Reece played with his mug of coffee and stared at the pieces on his chessboard. He'd beaten Dr Jaqui Ford three times and she'd beaten him five.

He was going out of his mind.

The weather was perfect, and that was half the trouble. Enough rain meant no bushfires. No wind meant no dramas at sea. They were out of the holiday season so people weren't doing damned fool holiday things. Which meant Air-Sea Rescue was having a very quiet time.

'Aren't you glad?' Jaqui enquired.

'Why should I be glad? I joined the service for excitement.'

'So you like people killing themselves?'

'I didn't mean that,' he growled. 'You know very well that I try my damnedest to stop people killing themselves. And you live on adrenaline just as much as I do.'

'Yes, but I have had a life,' Jaqui said mildly. 'Husband, kids, dogs. I come here for some peace. Yeah, I like the adrenaline rush of thinking we might be saving someone, but for the rest…work is my quiet time.'

Grady smiled at that. Jaqui was in her mid-fifties and was a very competent doctor. She'd only just undertaken the additional training to join Air-Sea Rescue, but already the tales of her tribe of hell-raising adult sons were legion. Everyone knew why Jaqui thought rescuing people in high drama was a quiet life.

'No, but you,' Jaqui said insistently. 'You can't depend on this for your excitement. Maybe you need kids of your own.'

'To provide me with drama? I don't think so.'

'So you're not into families?' Jaqui was probing past the

31

point of politeness, but Grady's associate was no respecter of boundaries.

'Not interested,' Grady growled, hoping to shut her up.

It didn't.

'You're not gay?'

That got a grin. 'What do you think?'

'You never know these days,' Jaqui said, moving her bishop with a nonchalance that told Grady she was hoping he might not notice she was threatening his queen. 'Someone once told me you can detect gayness if a man wears one earring, but my sons wear one, two or sixteen, depending on how the mood takes them. As they also seem to have one, two or sixteen girlfriends, depending on how the mood takes them, who would know anything at all? So…' She sat back and subjected him to intense scrutiny. 'Not gay. Not seriously involved. There's never been a woman who looked like being long term?'

'Cut it out.'

'Max told me you were really smitten once. A lady called Morag.'

Max was their pilot. Max talked too much.

'Morag and I went out for about a month. Four years ago.'

'Was that all? I thought it was serious.'

Maybe it was, Grady thought ruefully. He'd hardly thought through the consequences at the time but after she'd gone…he'd missed her like hell. Not that there'd been any choice in the matter. She'd buried herself in some remote little settlement and that surely wasn't the life for him.

So what? Why was he thinking of Morag now? he asked himself. He'd moved on. He'd dated. Morag had been a one-month relationship followed up by a letter of sympathy after her sister had died. It had been an intense letter that had taken him a long time to draft, but she'd never answered. So…

So one of these days a lady would come on the scene who'd make him smile as Morag had made him smile. But with no attachments.

'You don't want kids?' Jaqui asked.

'Why would I want kids?'

'You want excitement. Kids equal excitement.'

'I'll get my excitement some other way,' he growled. He moved his queen, removed his hand from the board and then saw the danger. 'Whoops. Check.'

'Checkmate,' Jaqui said sweetly, and then looked up as Max came through the door. One look at their pilot's face and they knew there were to be no more chess matches that afternoon.

'What is it?'

'Code One,' Max said shortly. 'Huge. We're going in first, with back-up on the way. The army'll be in on this, but, Grady, you've been put in charge first off. Tsunami.'

'A tidal wave,' Jaqui said incredulously. 'Where?'

'Petrel Island. Contact to the island's completely cut. The first reports have come in from fishing boats that were out to sea when the wave hit. All we know is that there were five hundred inhabitants on the island when a wall of water twenty feet high swept through. God knows how many are left alive.'

It was ten minutes before Morag met anyone at all. She was climbing down as people were climbing up, but the shortest way to high ground wasn't the track she was on. So her path was deserted. At every step she took her dread increased.

Finally she reached the town's outskirts, and here she met Marcus. Marcus was the head of the town's volunteer fire brigade, a brilliant fisherman and a man who normally could be absolutely depended on in a crisis. He looked…lost.

'Marcus…'

He was at the top of the track she was taking into town, the road leading to the fire station. Or it was the track that *had* led to the fire station. Marcus was standing where the station had once stood. The flimsy shed had given way completely, and a pile of rubble covered the town's only fire engine.

Marcus was staring unseeingly at the mess, and he didn't turn as Morag touched his shoulder.

'I don't know where they are,' he whispered, turning to gaze down at the ruined township.

He was soaked. He'd been caught by the wave, Morag thought, stunned, which meant the water must have washed almost three hundred yards inland. A shallow gash ran down the side of his face, and he looked as sick as she felt.

But they weren't alone. Above the township was bushland and the bush seemed the extreme of the wave's reach. Morag turned and looked upward and here was the first good news. People were emerging. They were still obviously terrified, but they were slowly venturing out.

All eyes were still turned toward the sea.

'Marcus!' It was a cry of disbelief—of tremulous joy. A woman was running toward them, towing two seemingly scared-witless teenagers after her. Judy. Marcus's wife. Marcus's face went slack with relief, and so did Morag's.

This was Marcus's family. With Marcus behind her she might get something organised, and now he had his family safe she could start.

Something…

What?

First things first. She had to wait until Marcus had gathered Judy and the kids to him in the hug of a man who'd thought he'd lost everything.

Finally he released them and turned to Morag. 'S-sorry.'

'Don't be sorry,' Morag said unsteadily. 'I wouldn't mind if someone hugged me.'

Judy immediately obliged. Marcus added his mite. Teenage dignity forgotten, the kids joined in, too, until she was squeezed between the four of them. And suddenly she was sobbing like a child.

Two minutes were spent gathering herself, taking strength where she most needed it.

Then…as they finally, tentatively broke away from each other and turned to stare out to sea again, they found space to talk.

'There's not likely to be another, is there?' Marcus asked, and Morag tried to think clearly about the possibility.

'I don't know. Maybe. Hubert and Robbie are on lookout with the bell, and Robbie has the best eyes on the island.'

'Was it you who rang the bell?' Judy asked, and when Morag nodded she was hugged all over again.

'Thank God for you, girl. There we all were, like sitting ducks, huddled in the main street waiting to be washed away.'

'Who was left behind?'

'God knows,' Marcus said frankly. 'I was just climbing into the fire truck, thinking after the tremor I'd pull it clear in case it was needed. I heard your bell, but I was trying to get the engine started. It seemed…important. Then as the bell kept ringing I came out—just as the water surged up. I ran. Even so, I had to grab a fence or I'd have been washed away. Judy, you…'

'I was with most of them,' Judy told them. She was still clutching the kids—Wendy, aged fourteen, and Jake, who was sixteen. Normally they wouldn't be seen dead clutching their mother but they were clutching her just as much as she was clutching them. 'Most of us got to the bush. If we made it to safety, then I'd guess most people would have. Then I thought you'd be at the fire station, Marcus, so I came.' She hugged her husband again, and her teenagers hugged, too.

'There must be casualties,' Morag whispered, and Marcus nodded.

'Yeah. Thank God it's Sunday so the school's empty.'

The school was on the foreshore. The thought of what might have happened—and hadn't—was almost enough to steady her.

'OK.' Deep breath. Somehow she had to figure out a way forward, though the extent of the calamity was overpowering. But she had four able-bodied people—five, counting herself— and, by the sound of it, the bulk of the townsfolk were safe. She needed to gear up. She needed to think.

'Let's get everyone safe first,' she told them. 'The cricket ground is on high ground and we can set up the pavilion as a clearing house. Marcus, I want you and Jake to start a house-to-house search—get others involved if you can—and send everyone to the cricket ground. I want *everyone* settled on high ground as fast as possible. Judy, I want you to make a register so we can see who's missing. Every person has to report to you.'

She paused and gazed across the village where she could see the roof of her tiny, four-bed hospital. Thankfully it was on high ground but she knew at once that it'd be too small for what lay ahead. Plus, even though it was on high ground, it was low enough for a higher wave to do damage. It'd have to be evacuated.

'I'll set up a medical centre in the cricket pavilion,' she told them. 'On the way I'll go past the hospital and make sure everyone's out and safe. Judy, can you and Wendy come with me and help me carry things? I need supplies, plus the files holding every islander's records. Wendy, are you able to cross-match names with the list Judy's making?' She gave them all a tiny, watery smile. 'I know. I'm sounding bossy when all we want to do is hug each other. But we need to move. Marcus, that cut—'

'Can wait,' he said roughly. 'I've a feeling that's the least of our problems.'

As if on cue, there was a yell from below them. An elderly man—the village grocer—was running toward them, and his terror reached them before he did.

'Doc. Doc, thank God you're safe. Doc, Mavis got caught under water. She's so cold and limp… Oh, God, Doc… She looks awful. I've taken her to the clinic but there's no one there who can help. Can you come?'

Morag started work right then, and she didn't raise her head for hours.

So many injuries… She didn't know how many injuries. She could only focus on what was before her.

She worked first at the clinic, as that was where Mavis was.

Morag worked over Mavis with fierce intensity, blotting out
the sound of evacuation going on all around her, and blotting
out the fact that another wave could come at any time.

But despite her best efforts, the outcome was tragedy.
There'd been twenty minutes between immersion and the time
Morag saw the elderly grocer's wife. When Morag reached her,
one of the nurses had started CPR but it was no use. The ECG
tracing showed idioventricular rhythm. Idioventricular rhythm
was almost always irreversible—the last sigh of a dying
heart—and this was no exception. Finally Morag stood back,
defeated, and she put her arm around the grocer's shoulders in
silent sympathy as he wept for his wife.

But there was no time for Morag to weep. The clinic was
almost empty. Every patient and almost all the equipment was
gone. They covered Mavis and left her there.

'This…this place can be the morgue,' she told one of the
men who'd tried to help.

He nodded. 'We'll start bringing them in.'

Them? How many? She couldn't bear to ask. 'I need to
see…to make sure…'

'If there's any doubt at all, we'll bring them to you,' he told
her. 'But there's those…well, there's those where there's no
doubt at all.'

Dear God.

Grim-faced, Morag made her way to the cricket pavilion.
Here she found her surgery set up in miniature. Any villager
not totally occupied with searching for survivors or helping the
injured had been hauled in to help. Marcus and his family were
working like a miniature army.

There was no time to wonder. Work was waiting everywhere.

Louise, a middle-aged nurse who usually acted as Morag's
receptionist, had decreed herself triage sister and nothing got
near Morag unless she said so. That meant Morag nearly
missed seeing tiny Orlando Salmon. Her next tragedy.

Orlando had been held in his mother's arms when the water

had slammed them from one side of the road to the other. Angie Salmon was left with bruising, but her tiny son was dead in her arms. Louise would have deflected her from Morag— Morag had so much on her hands that the clearly dead could no longer be her business—but Morag saw them out of the corner of her eye as she was treating a compound fracture, and the look on Angie's face had her move instinctively to help.

Once again, there was nothing constructive she could do. But Angie had to hear from a doctor that her little son was really dead. She had to watch as Morag took the time to examine the tiny child with love, and show Angie what had killed him. It had been fast. He'd died instantly in his mother's arms.

Explaining was all Morag could do, and it was all she had time for. There was no time for comfort. There were urgent cases waiting, but as Morag turned away she found herself choked again with tears. She and Angie had gone to school together. Angie had been the biggest tomboy on the island. She had four more kids, and each one was loved to bits.

Damn.

She needed Robbie, she thought bleakly. She desperately needed to hug her own little Robbie, but there was no time.

And she was depending on Robbie. They all were. He was the village eyes. Someone else had gone up on the ridge now, carrying the strongest field glasses they could find, but she knew that Robbie's sharp eyes would be behind those glasses.

Searching for another wave.

She couldn't think of another wave.

Morag worked and worked. Every time she turned around there was more need. Fractures, lacerations, grief…

Then about four hours after the water hit, they brought Sam Crane in, carrying him in on a brightly painted door that looked like it had once been entry point to one of the village's more substantial houses.

Louise saw Sam as the stretcher bearers reached the top of the stairs, and this time she had no hesitation in bringing him to Morag's immediate attention. Morag turned from the man she'd been treating and flinched. Dear heaven. So much blood.

'We found him round the back of the harbour,' Marcus told her. 'He was working on his boat when it hit. The boat ended up smashed on the harbour wall and we found him underneath. It's taken six of us to get the boat off him. As soon as we got the boat off, he started bleeding like a stuck pig. We've applied pressure but...'

But what? She was lifting the rough blanket way, searching for the source of the bleeding. And here it was.

'Boat crushed his leg,' Marcus told her. 'What'll we do?'

His leg was lost. That much was unmistakable. What was left was a mash of pulp and splintered bones. The only positive thing was that his leg had been crushed so thoroughly that the blood vessels themselves must have been crushed. With a wound like this she'd expect spurting blood and almost immediate death, but somehow, hours after the wave, he was still alive.

Not for long, though. Blood was oozing across the door and onto the pavilion floor.

'We need blood. Plasma. Saline.'

'We're just about out.' Irene, the island's midwife, turned from applying a pressure bandage to a small boy's thigh. 'I could use some here.'

'We need to set up a blood bank.' Morag was staring down at Sam's leg in dismay. She had two trained nurses: Louise and Irene. That meant there were three people with medical skills on the entire island. That was it. How could she cope with this? Sam needed his leg amputated right now if he was to live—but she had no anaesthetist. Her nurses would be needed to take blood. The sort of surgery she was envisaging was horrific, but if she didn't start now, Sam would die almost straight away.

Triage. Priorities. Someone else was calling out for her from below. The child Irene was working on really needed Morag's attention. Maybe Sam would have to be...

'Just cut it off, Doc,' Sam said weakly, reaching out and taking her hand. 'I know it's a mess. I can get by on one leg.'

'You can do anything, Sam,' she said in a voice that wasn't the least bit steady. She gripped Sam's hand and she wasn't sure who was gaining strength from who. 'Sam, I'm going to give you enough painkiller to block things out until we can sort out how best to cope with this.'

'But the leg has to come of?'

'Yes, Sam. The leg has to come off.'

'Let's get on with it, then.'

'Sure.' She loaded a syringe and injected morphine. She set up an IV line and watched as Sam drifted into sleep. Or unconsciousness. The combination of shock, blood loss and morphine meant he could no longer stay with them.

Irene was watching her. As Sam's hand loosened its grip and she stepped back, she found everyone was watching her.

The huddle of people in the pavilion were shocked past belief. Any islander who was fit and not needed to take care of their own family had been co-opted into helping with medical care. But in this tiny settlement everyone knew everyone, and the entire island was like an extended family.

So far the death count from this afternoon was ten and rising. They'd worked so far in numbed disbelief but suddenly that numbness had disappeared. Every single one of them knew what Morag was facing now.

She needed to turn away from Sam and give her attention to someone she could save.

She needed to give up on the impossible.

She couldn't. She just…couldn't.

'Irene, if I talk you through the anaesthetic…' she managed, and Irene nodded.

'I'll try.'

They both knew it was hopeless.

'Is this the medical centre?'

The voice from down on the cricket ground was strong and insistent, different to the frantic cries for help they'd been hearing. Morag turned, momentarily distracted, knowing she'd reached the end of her resources.

But this was no islander calling for help. They'd been so caught up in the appalling drama that no one had noticed the approach of a small group of yellow-overalled outsiders.

Outsiders.

Help.

Morag looked down at the cluster of people below her. They looked unreal. Like aliens from space. Every islander was mud-coated, battered and torn, either from their own meeting with the wave or from hauling others from the rubble. But these newcomers were clean, purposeful, dressed to work and work hard.

Where had they come from?

'The helicopter,' someone whispered. 'The fishing boats radioed the mainland for help. A helicopter landed ten minutes back.'

Morag hadn't heard any helicopter, but she had been so focused on urgent need that she'd heard nothing.

She stared down at the group of six. From this distance she couldn't tell what sex they were—who they were—but they were the first glimmer of the outside world. The first glimmer of sanity.

'Is anyone a doctor?' she called without much hope, but a tall, yellow-overalled figure separated from the bunch and strode up the stairs three at a time.

'I'm a doctor and so is Jaqui,' he called as he climbed. 'Ron and Elsey are paramedics and Doug's here to assess priorities so we can get the personnel we need from the mainland. Who's in charge?' His words were cutting through the confusion and the chaos, and his tone was measured to command.

'I guess I am,' Morag said unsteadily, glanced despairingly down at Sam. 'If you're a doctor…I need help. So much help…'

'You have it.' The man passed the group clustered round Sam's wife at the head of the stairs—and she looked up from

Sam and saw who it was at almost exactly the moment he registered who it was he was talking to.

Morag saw shock—absolute stunned amazement. His amazement matched hers, and then she couldn't register any expression on his face at all.

Just for a moment her vision blurred. Just for a moment her knees sagged.

Then Grady was beside her. His arms were holding her against him, and just for a moment she let herself give way. The shock and horror and fear of the last three hours all culminated in this one moment of total weakness. This man was here where she'd never imagined. At such a moment.

Grady…

Enough. Of course it was Grady. Why should she be shocked? Grady was always dashing to Australia's disaster areas. That was what he did.

This was a disaster. He was here.

'Three deep breaths,' Grady was saying into her hair. 'Hell, Morag, I'd forgotten… But you're not by yourself. We're the forerunners, but there's massive help on the way. Tell me what needs to be done most urgently.'

She heard him. She took the three deep breaths he'd advised while she permitted herself the luxury of sagging against his chest. Feeling his strength. Feeling for this one moment that indeed she wasn't alone.

Then she regrouped. She hauled herself away. She looked up at him and searched his face and she saw the same implacable strength she'd seen in him four years before.

And his strength fed hers. The islanders were gazing at her with dismay. If she disintegrated they all could, their expressions said, and this one show of weakness had to be her last.

'We've set this up as command centre,' she managed. 'There are teams combing the island, trying to account for every islander. Ten confirmed deaths so far. Multiple casualties. But we can't cope. We've run out of every medical necessity. This is our last bag of saline. I'm out of morphine. Bandages.

Everything.' She swallowed and turned to Sam. 'Priority here is Sam's leg.'

Grady had already seen. He moved her aside and checked the IV line. Lifted Sam's wrist.

Looked down at the mangled leg.

'I'm operating now,' Morag said, and he nodded, a half-smile twisting his craggy face.

'Of course you are. All by yourself.' Then he turned away to the yellow overalls following him up the stairs. 'We need operating facilities now,' he called. 'Urgent. Elsey, get saline, plasma, everything we need for major surgery right now. Bring it all up here from the chopper. Morag, don't worry about supplies. We came fully loaded for medical emergencies. Max, we need lighting. Jaqui, will you do the anaesthetic? I'll operate and Morag here will assist. Rod, can you help with the child's thigh, there? He looks like he needs an IV line and pain relief. Tell me what his blood pressure is. Morag, is there anything else that's as urgent as Sam?'

In one broad sweep he'd assessed the chaos. Leaving her speechless. 'No,' she managed. 'Not…not yet.'

He nodded. 'The first Chinook will be landing in the next half-hour,' he told her. 'The army's sending troops. We aim to have everyone accounted for by nightfall. Meanwhile, let's cope with this and face the rest of the mess afterwards.'

It was a dreadful operation, done in the most primitive of conditions. Removing a man's leg, even a leg as dreadfully injured as this, was nothing less than butchering. Morag had seen it done—had assisted before with patients with tumours or with complications from diabetes—and each time the operation had made her feel ill. How much more so now when her world was spinning out of control?

And yet…it was in control again—a little—because of this man. Grady was good. There was no one she'd rather have in this emergency than Grady. Once the emergency lights were set up, he went straight in.

They were using the door as an operating table. There was no screening from the rest of the people using the pavilion. Sterility of the environment was a joke. But it couldn't be allowed to matter. Grady moved with care, blocking out all else.

He took the leg off just above the knee. He tied off damaged blood vessels, working carefully, quickly and skilfully.

Finally the bleeding eased, and by the time the remains of the fisherman's leg could be removed and taken away for burial, everyone there knew that Sam had a fighting chance at life. And this had been no butchering job. The remains of the leg were viable. He'd have a stump which could be used as a basis for an artificial limb. The operation couldn't have been done much better if it had been done in a major city hospital.

For the first time, Morag felt the wash of hopelessness recede. Sam had suffered massive blood loss, but if he was going to go into cardiac arrest, surely it would have happened sooner. Now they had saline and plasma flowing at maximum rate, and Jaqui was watching his breathing like a hawk.

Jaqui might look an unlikely doctor—a middle-aged woman, almost six feet tall, skinny and shiny in her canary yellow overalls—but there was no doubting her skills as an anaesthetist. The bleeding had been stemmed and the otherwise healthy fisherman now had a chance to fight back.

Finally, as Grady worked over the dressing, Morag found herself with time to step away. For the first time since she'd seen that awful wall of water, she had time to assimilate what had happened.

Marcus was standing behind her. The big fisherman was waiting in the shadows, as if he, too, was taking a breather from the horror he'd been working with. She stepped back to him, taking in his shocked and haggard face. She knew her own face must mirror it.

'What's happening?'

'The world's arrived,' he told her in a voice that was barely audible. It was as if every ounce of strength had been sucked out of him with the shock. 'The chopper that these people came in on was a forerunner. Two Chinook helicopters full of army personnel are here now, using the paddock up the top of the fells as a landing base. Teams are searching the island. There's boats out to sea, still searching.'

'People are still missing?'

He lifted a piece of paper and stared down, unseeing. She followed his eyes and flicked through the names—and winced.

'The Koori community are missing about eight of their people,' he told her. 'They were on the beach. They saw the water being sucked out and went to get a closer look. They ended up being washed everywhere. Lots of lacerations but some of their kids… And some of ours…' His voice broke and Morag put her arms around him and hugged. Hard.

And tried not to think about a name she'd seen on the list.

'We can get through this, Marcus,' she said softly. 'But we can't break. Not you and I. Too much depends on us.'

'You're right.' He wiped his face on the back of his sleeve and his face tightened. 'You're bloody right, Doc. I'll be out again in a bit, but I just came to see how Sam was going.'

'He'll make it. Thanks to these people.'

'Yeah, it's a good thing there's an outside world,' Marcus said grimly. 'And maybe it's the only thing left to us. I've seen the town. The houses…'

'Don't think about it.' She glanced back at the table to where Jaqui and Grady were still working. They could do without her now. It was almost sunset. It was time to move on to her next priority. 'Marcus, I need to see to the lighthouse. What if the light's not working? And I need to see Robbie. He'll be frantic.'

'Yeah, you go, lass,' he told her. 'With two doctors here, they should be able to manage. You carrying your radio?'

She gestured to it on her belt. 'Always.'

'You'll need to walk,' he told her. 'Most of the roads are washed out.'

'Yeah, and I'd imagine my car is floating somewhere in the Pacific.' She shrugged. 'I can walk. I can even run. But…'

Marcus saw her hesitation and had no trouble identifying it.

'I've been on the line to some expert from Sydney. The Centre for Seismology or some such. She says the wave was from the shock caused by the earthquake. She also says the epicentre was miles from here. There were two smaller waves after the big one but they've settled. The scientists are on full alert for any more shocks, but she says more waves are incredibly unlikely—and even if they happen, we'll now get heaps of warning.'

'So we're safe?'

'Yeah. Sort of. Robbie's been watching all afternoon but he's off duty now.'

She managed a smile. 'The whole island's been dependent on a nine- and a ninety-year-old. My guess is that Hubert won't choose to die this week.'

'I surely hope not. We've had enough deaths.' Marcus's smile matched hers—weak and with no life behind it. 'OK.' He shrugged. 'I need to go. I shouldn't have come, but I couldn't bear to leave Sam.'

'He stands every chance of recovering.' Morag glanced once more over her shoulder to where Grady was completing his work. He had no attention to spare for her, and she had none to spare for him.

But he was here. The thought was overwhelming in the measure of comfort it gave her. This afternoon had been her worst kind of nightmare, and she was taking any vestige of comfort wherever she could find it. So she let herself look at Grady for a moment longer, taking in the solid competency, his air of command, the presence he exuded without ever seeming aware of it.

Enough. She was being silly. His presence was a comfort but there was nothing more to be done here.

'Let's go,' she told Marcus—and she turned away from Grady to follow Marcus, out of the cricket pavilion and into the mess of the island that had once been their home.

CHAPTER FOUR

THE lighthouse was a priority.

Morag had two jobs on the island. One was island doctor, the other was lighthouse-keeper, and who could say which was more important? They both saved lives.

Once, being lighthouse-keeper had been a full-time job, but now it was simply a matter of ensuring that the light was still functioning, and that was a vastly different task than in the days when kerosene had had to be carted up the tower every night. Now the light was powered by electricity, with solar back-up.

Normally an alarm would sound if the light was dimmed in any way, but the alarm was in the lighthouse-keeper's cottage. Morag's home. And the cottage was at the foot of the lighthouse, not high enough above sea level to avoid damage.

It had been early afternoon when the wave had struck. Now the last rays of sun were sinking over the horizon and the darkness caused more problems. The streets were a mess, the streetlights were history, and a walk that usually took five minutes took her half an hour.

She made her way along the devastated main street, skirting the massive build-up of clutter smashed there by the water, clambering over piles of what had been treasured possessions but were now sodden garbage, stopping occasionally to speak to people searching through the mess that had once been their homes.

People stopped her all the time. People were desperate to make contact, to talk through what had happened.

But there was no longer an urgent medical need for her. Grady and his people were coping with medical needs for now, and she had to move on.

She must. The light…

She came to the end of the street and turned from the shelter of the ruined buildings onto the tiny, wind-swept promontory that held the lighthouse.

The lighthouse itself was still standing. Of course. It was built of stone, built to withstand massive seas, built to cope with anything nature threw at it.

The cottage, though…

She stood and stared, seeing not the ruins of the whitewashed building that had been her home for the last four years but seeing what it had once held.

Robbie's memories. Photographs of Beth and her husband. Robbie's precious teddy, knitted for him by his mother when she'd been so ill she'd hardly been able to hold needles. The furniture carved by Morag's father, splintered, ruined…

The lighthouse. Concentrate on the lighthouse. She choked back tears and looked up to find the light blinking its warning into the dusk.

At least one thing in this dysfunctional world was still working to order.

She stared upward for a long time. Stay away from here, the light was saying. The light was supposed to be warning ships that here were rocks to be wary of, but this day the danger had come from the sea itself, and the wreck was inland.

Her home was ruined.

She'd have to find Robbie.

She turned away, blinded by tears, and someone was standing in her path.

Grady.

Grady was right…there.

'They told me you'd come here,' he said, in that serious voice she'd known and loved all those years ago. A lifetime ago. He was looking down at her in the half-dark and it was all she could do not to fall on his chest again. Only, of course, she couldn't. How could she? And why would she? Sure, this was a tragedy, but it was her tragedy. It had nothing to do with this man.

He was here because it was his job to be here, she thought bleakly. He had nothing to do with her.

'Aren't you needed back at the pavilion?' she asked, and his gaze didn't falter.

'I thought I might be needed here. With you.'

'There's nothing to do here. The light's still working.'

'You really are the lighthouse-keeper?'

'Like father, like daughter. Yes.'

'Morag, I'm sorry.'

She had no idea what he was sorry for. So many things... She had no idea where he intended to start.

'Don't be sorry,' she said. 'It doesn't help.'

'This is your house?' He gazed at the battered whitewashed buildings. The light was fading fast now, and the beam from the lighthouse was becoming more obvious, one brief, hard beam out over the waves each fifteen seconds. The waves were washing gently over the rocks, their soft lapping making a mockery of the wave that had come before.

From where they stood you couldn't see around the headland into the town. The ruins were hardly apparent—unless you stared into the smashed windows of the cottage and saw the chaos that had been her home.

'Do you need to do anything for the lighthouse?' he asked, and she shook her head.

'No. The electricity's cut but we have solar power back-up. The solar panels on the cottage roof seem to be just under the high-water mark, and the connections must still be intact. That was what I was most worried about. I needed to check that the light was OK.'

'To stop further tragedy?'

'Without the light...yes, there'd be further tragedy.' She gazed across the great white tower, following its lines down to where it was anchored on solid rock. 'It doesn't look harmed. One wave couldn't wash it away. Unlike...'

'Unlike the rest of the island.' He hesitated, watching her face as she turned again to face the wreckage of her home. 'It was some wave.'

'It was the most frightening thing I've ever seen,' she whispered. 'I thought everyone would be dead. I couldn't believe that so many would live. But still...there's so much...' She let herself think of the lists Marcus had held—and the name that among them all had her cringing the most. Doctors shouldn't get personal, she thought. Ha!

Somewhere there was a little boy called Hamish. Robbie's best friend.

Enough. The little boy had probably been found by now, and even if he hadn't, she couldn't let herself think past a point where madness seemed to beckon. She gathered herself tight, allowing anger to replace distress. 'Why aren't you back at the pavilion? I wouldn't have left if I thought you and Jaqui weren't staying.'

'We have things under control and I can get back fast if I'm needed,' he told her. He was still watching her face. 'There's two doctors on the Chinook—the helicopter we're using to evacuate the worst of the wounded. We're evacuating those now. Peter and Christine Rafferty. Iris Helgin. Ross Farr. You've done a great job, Morag, but multiple fractures and internal injuries need specialist facilities.'

She nodded. 'How about Lucy Rafferty?' she asked tightly. 'Did she go with her parents?' Peter and Christine had been badly hurt—Peter with a badly fractured leg and Christine with concussion as well as fractures, but their thirteen-year-old daughter hadn't seemed as badly hurt.

And their son? Hamish? She thought the question but she didn't add it out loud.

'We didn't have room for Lucy,' Grady was saying. 'And we thought—'

She nodded, cutting him off. She knew what he thought.

'And Sam?' she managed. He could hear how involved she was, she thought. He must do.

But so what? she demanded of herself. The medical imperative—not to get personally involved—how on earth could she ever manage that here?

'You can't act at peak professional level if your emotions get in the way,' she'd been taught in medical school, and she wondered what her examiners would think of the way she was reacting now.

Well, it was too late to fail her. They were welcome to try.

'We're making sure Sam's stable before we transfer him,' Grady was saying. 'But he'll make it. I'm sure he'll make it.'

'Without his leg,' she whispered. 'No more fishing.'

'But still a life.'

'Maybe.' She stared again at the ruins of her cottage. The water had smashed its way everywhere. Through gaps where once there'd been window-panes, she could see a mass of sand and mud and sludge a yard deep.

Where to start…

Robbie.

Hamish. Dear God.

'I need to find my nephew,' she said bleakly.

'Beth's child?'

'Yes.'

'Where is he?' Grady asked, and then added, more urgently, 'Morag, do you know where he is?'

What was he thinking? she thought incredulously. That she'd only now thought of the little boy's whereabouts?

'Of course I know where he is,' she snapped. 'I never would have left him if he hadn't been safe. I would have stayed. But I had to go. Sam…Hamish…the others. But Hubert will take care…'

She wasn't making sense, even to herself. Grady looked at her, his face intent and serious in the fading light.

'So he's with someone called Hubert. Where's Hubert?'

'Up on the ridge above the town. Hubert's cottage is the high point of the island. I was up there when…'

'When you saw the wave,' Grady said. 'You were very

lucky. Marcus told me what happened. If it hadn't been for your quick thinking…'

'Yeah, if I hadn't been here,' she said, and it was impossible to keep the bitterness from her voice. 'If I hadn't been where I belonged, we'd all be dead. But I was. Now, if you'll excuse me, Grady, I need to find my nephew.'

'I'll come with you.'

'No.'

'Yes,' he said, and he took her hand, whether she liked it or not. 'You're as much a victim as anyone else on this island, Morag. Your home is in ruins. You possess only the clothes you stand up in. You're shocked and you're exhausted. I'm taking you in charge. We'll go up together and fetch Robbie and then I'll take you to the tents they're setting up on the cricket grounds to care for all of you. Learn to accept help, Morag. You'll have to take it over the next few weeks, like it or not.'

She stared at him. Helpless. Lost. And when he held her hand tighter, she didn't pull away.

She was going to need this man over the next few weeks? Right. She did need him.

The only problem was that it wasn't just for now. She'd needed him for four long years and that need had never faded.

She'd needed him then and she needed him desperately now.

Grady.

Her love.

It was all a mist, she thought. A delirious dream where horror and death and Grady and love—and sheer unmitigated hopelessness—all mingled.

They had to walk up the fells, scrambling up the scree to Hubert's cottage. The goat track was hard to find in the dim light. Grady had a flashlight and it picked out the path.

He held onto her hand all the way. To do otherwise seemed stupid. The fact that his touch made her sense of unreality deepen couldn't be allowed to matter.

Maybe she should release herself from his grip, she thought inconsequentially. She wasn't nervous of the dark. Brought up to know every nook and cranny on the island, Morag was as at home here as she was in the city on a well-lit street. Grady needed the flashlight but she let her feet move automatically.

Dear heaven, this was so dreadful…

The thought of Angie kept filling her vision. Angie's tiny cold baby. And Mavis. And so many dead…

And Hamish?

No.

She couldn't think. Somehow she blocked her thoughts until the only thing she was aware of was the presence of this man beside her.

It helped. It stopped her getting her head around what had happened this day.

So much had happened since she'd last walked up here that Morag was having trouble believing that any of this was real. This afternoon she'd strolled up the path with Robbie by her side, happy because it was a glorious Sunday afternoon and the island was the best place to be in the entire world. Robbie had kicked his soccer ball along in front of him, letting it roll down the scree, whooping and hollering and occasionally returning to her side to keep up his latest plea for a puppy.

'Please, Morag. We need a puppy. We need a dog. We need…'

Then there'd been the talk of Elspeth.

I wonder how many island dogs have survived? she thought, and then thought even more savagely, I wonder how many dogs need new owners?

Her head was right back into the tragedy. How could she escape it?

'It'll be OK.'

'How can it be all right?' she said into the night, not really talking to Grady. She was talking to herself. 'How can things be righted? So much destroyed…'

'The chopper pilot on the way over said there'd been talk

of resettling the islanders,' Grady said cautiously. 'Making this an unpopulated island. With so much of the infrastructure damaged, maybe that'd be the way to go.'

Oh, right. Smash homes and then rip the island out from under them.

'Yeah, the government would like that,' she said bitterly. 'It costs them an arm and a leg in support—to have ships drop off supplies, to provide things like mail, telecommunications, health services...'

'You *are* the health services.'

'I know, and if I wasn't here they'd close the island in a minute,' she told him. 'They've decided again that the lighthouse can manage unmanned. They don't want to provide infrastructure and it drives the powers that be nuts that I agreed to stay here. I'm the only reason this island can function.' She shook herself, trying to lose the feeling of nightmarish unreality. 'And now there'll be more pressure. How the hell can we rebuild? All these people? There'll be so many problems. I can't cope...'

'Hey, Morag.' His hand tightened on hers, holding her, steadying her as she stumbled along a track which all of a sudden wasn't as familiar as she'd thought. And, dammit, she was too far gone to pull away. Sure, it was his bedside manner doing the comforting, but she needed any bedside manner she could get.

Liar. She needed Grady.

Whatever.

She'd deal with the consequences later, she told herself dully. For tonight—for now—she needed Grady.

He held on and she gripped him tight in return, and she sensed in the sudden, momentary stillness that her reciprocation had surprised him.

'Morag...'

'Shut up,' she told him. 'I don't want to think about tomorrow. I just need to see Robbie. I need to focus on now. That's all I can do.'

*   *   *

There was a candle in Hubert's cottage window, lit in welcome.

The electricity for the entire island was cut. The outside teams had brought emergency generators which they were using at the cricket ground, and the lighthouse had its solar power, but the rest of the island was in darkness.

But Hubert had never had need of electricity and, though the rest of the island was in darkness, here was light. As they walked up to the door, Morag felt a sudden surge of affection for the old man who'd surely surpassed himself this day.

She entered without knocking, ushering Grady with her. Hubert was sitting at the kitchen table, fully dressed.

He hadn't been fully dressed for months, Morag thought, stunned. In his fishermen's ancient jersey and overalls, he looked far younger than the Hubert she'd treated that afternoon. He looked tough and competent and extremely worried.

As they entered his face cleared, just a little.

'I thought you'd never come, girl. Thank God for it.'

'This is Dr Reece,' she told Hubert, and then moved to her first concern. 'Robbie...'

'He's fine,' Hubert told her. 'Or he's as well as he can be. We both saw what happened and he knew you were all right. Chris Bartner brought his telescope up to the ridge, and we've seen everything that's happened since. But Robbie's scared for his mates. For Hamish. And my...for all our friends.'

Morag swallowed. 'I haven't gone over the lists in full.'

'The lists...' Hubert watched her face and then rose stiffly and crossed to the stove. He lifted the kettle and filled his blackened teapot. His niece would be waiting a while longer for her inheritance, Morag thought dully. Hubert's teapot was still very definitely needed.

Then—teapot full—Hubert nodded gravely across at Grady.

'If you're a doctor, then you must be one of the people who came in by the first helicopter. Thank God for you. Chris's wife came up half an hour back to tell us we could leave our watching, and she said our Sam would live, thanks to you.' He hesitated. 'But, Morag, I need to know. Chris's wife couldn't speak for weeping. Elias is… Elias *was* her grandfather, and her grandmother needed her badly. So Christopher took her away before she could tell me more. Lists or not, tell me what the damage is.'

So she told him. It still seemed totally unreal. Sitting at the scrubbed wooden table, eating sandwiches that Hubert had magically produced—she hadn't realised how hungry she was but now she ate without tasting—sipping hot, sugared tea, with Grady sitting beside her, Morag outlined the damage as she knew it.

All the houses along the seafront were damaged, some irreparably. The flimsier structures, such as the shed that had served as a fire station, had never stood a chance. Even some of the stronger-built houses had been smashed to firewood. There were twelve confirmed deaths now, mostly from those first awful minutes. Death by sheer smashing force or by drowning as people had been caught in rubble, unable to escape the water. Another six had been reported missing. So far. Not including the Koori population, and the initial reports from the settlement were disastrous. She needed to go out there.

She needed to do so much. So many missing…

Maybe the missing were still alive, she told herself. But maybe not. The more time passed, the more unlikely it was that anyone would be found.

But all the local boats were assisting in the search—boats that had, thankfully, been out at sea when the wave had struck. The local fishermen were now combing the coast, trying to find anyone or anything swept away.

That was the appalling news. That was the news that made Hubert's face grow grey, and Morag put out a hand, ostensibly to give him comfort but also to check his pulse…

There was more. Little things she'd learned without realising it came to her now as she sat between these very different men. The loss of Robbie's teddy. Pets. William Cray's border collie. William was a writer, who had made the island his solitary home. He considered himself an intellectual—a cut above the islanders. He kept to himself. Yet as she'd walked to the lighthouse, Morag had seen him sitting on the debris-strewn beach, sobbing in appalled disbelief.

His dog was nowhere.

And the injured and the missing… Among them…

No. She wasn't going down that road. She wouldn't say it unless she knew for sure.

'What'll we do?' Hubert whispered as Morag's voice finally trailed off. Grady had stayed silent, seeming to know that she needed to talk. By making it real, maybe she could take it out of the realms of nightmare. Maybe it could be something that was over.

But, of course, it wasn't.

'I don't know,' she told him. 'But… Thank you for caring for Robbie. I had to trust you.'

Her voice faltered and Grady's hand came across the table to touch her. One day four years ago she'd pulled away from this comfort. Not now. Now when she needed him so much.

His touch was light. Intuitively, he was letting her focus still on Hubert.

'You knew I wouldn't let you down,' Hubert told her, his voice becoming all at once fierce. He glanced across the table at Grady, and his old eyes were suddenly defiant. 'That's what this island is all about. We depend on each other. We're tight-knit. And we're not done yet. No blasted wave is going to smash away our community.'

He had realised the situation well before her, Morag thought. While she'd been down at sea level tending to medical imperatives, Hubert had sat up here caring for Robbie, watching for more waves and thinking through what this meant long term.

'It's not the first time Petrel Island's faced tragedy,' he told Grady, still fiercely, as if in Grady he saw the threat of the outside world. The threat of the end of this lifestyle. 'When I was a kid they were still remembering the *Bertha* that ran aground on the far point. My dad swam out that night and brought four souls ashore, but a hundred and sixty-eight drowned. Then, fifty years back, the diphtheria came through. We didn't have a doctor—no one on the island was vaccinated against anything—and there are twenty-five more in the grave-yard who died before their time.' He glanced from Grady, who he wasn't quite sure of, to Morag, who he was.

'You're a doctor and you try and save us all,' he told her. 'But there's always fate, girl and you can't rail about it. You take what comes.'

'You fight,' Morag said.

'Yeah, you fight, and that's what you've been doing today while I've cared for the bairn.' He shrugged and cradled his teacup some more. 'He's a good kid, Morag. He knew he couldn't go down. He knew he'd have to wait up here with me. Waiting's the hardest but we did it together. He's in my bed.' A crooked smile crossed his face. 'With Elspeth. The two of them are worn out with worrying. I reckon I just might have to put Robbie's name on Elspeth.'

'Elspeth is Hubert's golden retriever,' Morag told Grady. 'And here he is promising to leave her to Robbie when he dies. But…don't die tonight, will you, Hubert?'

'Can't,' Hubert said bluntly. 'Someone else is in my bed. You want to join him? It's a big bed.'

Morag flashed an unsure glance at Grady. 'I…'

'You look stuffed to me,' Hubert told her. 'What do you reckon, fella?' He jabbed Grady in the chest. 'You agree you're capable of seeing that our girl is done in?'

'She is,' Grady said seriously. 'There's beds being set up in tents on the cricket ground.'

'Do they need her there now?'

Grady glanced at his watch. 'Maybe not,' he conceded. 'The urgent medical cases have been seen, the worst have been evac-uated and Jaqui's there now in case more problems arise. We'll take it in turns to sleep and she'll call us if she needs us.'

'Then, barring complications, you can both get some shut-eye up here,' Hubert said in satisfaction.

Morag gazed across the table in wonder at this dying old man who suddenly wasn't anywhere near dying. He seemed like a man in charge. 'Hubert, you're the one who's sick.'

'I'm still dying,' Hubert said morosely. 'But I'm not sick. There's a difference.'

'Why are you dying?' Grady asked, startled, and Hubert snorted.

''Cos I'm ninety-two and it's time. They've taken my cray-pot licences off me. But, as Morag says, not tonight. Now… there's a couple of them camp stretcher things in the shed and there's a heap of bedding and it's not a cold night. Morag, you slide into bed with the little fella. He'll be real glad to see you when he wakes—that wave was the stuff of nightmares. Me and the mainland doc will settle down here unless you're needed. You both have your radios on?'

'We do.' Morag was struggling to think, though in truth she couldn't. Her mind was so addled she was past thinking. The idea of sliding into bed with Robbie and holding him close was overwhelming.

Staying up here had much more appeal over going down to the huge tents they were setting up on the cricket ground— trying to sleep where everyone would be wanting to talk to her. And to sleep knowing that Grady was nearby…that the re- sponsibility had been lifted from her shoulders… It was an unlooked-for blessing and she could no sooner refuse it than fly. She glanced uncertainly across the table at Grady, and the hand touching hers moved so he was covering her hand en- tirely.

'I can't take your bed,' she told Hubert, forcing herself to concentrate on something other than the feel of Grady's hand.

'It's already taken,' Hubert told her. 'Don't be daft. I've spent half my life sleeping in fishing boats, sometimes on bare deck. The bairn's already asleep. Don't argue.'

But… 'Can we stay here?' she asked.

Grady was watching her, his face calm. He saw what she

was thinking, this man. Of course. He'd always been able to see.

'I think we can,' he said gently. 'Hubert's idea is excellent. I'll radio in and let my team know what's happening. If we're wanted, they'll call us. But you're exhausted, close to dropping. We all need to sleep. There's nothing else to be done until dawn.'

'How can I sleep in Hubert's bed?'

'Hey, I put clean sheets on,' Hubert growled. 'Elspeth's even warmed your side up. Why can't you?'

Because he was her patient, she thought, torn between tears of exhaustion and a sudden inexplicable need to laugh. This afternoon she'd been treating him. To have him suddenly rise from his deathbed and say, Here, I've put clean sheets on the bed; you take a turn…

'Hey, and deathbed or not, you're not allowed to die in it either,' Hubert told her, and he grinned. It was the first time she'd seen a smile since the wave had struck, and it felt good. Like the world was finally starting to settle.

Grady was smiling too, the smile she remembered so well from all those years ago, a smile that twisted her heart.

'Go and find Robbie, Morag,' he said, in the gentle tone she remembered him using with her once before. But this time was different. This time she grasped the comfort of his tone and she held on. It was warmth in a world where there wasn't warmth. It was hope.

'Go and sleep,' he said gently. 'Hubert and I will be right here, watching over you. You've done the work of a small army today. Now let someone else take care of you for a change.'

'But—'

'Goodnight, Morag. Go to sleep.'

Grady lay on the camp stretcher beside Hubert, but sleep wouldn't come.

The camp bed with no mattress was as hard as nails but he

didn't mind that. It wasn't discomfort that was keeping him awake. There'd been one mattress, which he'd insisted the old man have. 'For heaven's sake, man, I'm trained to sleep in a harness hanging off a cliff face if I must,' he'd told him, and it was the truth.

He'd trained himself over the years to snatch any sleep that was available. He needed sleep now. Jaqui knew what he was doing up here was important, and he'd organised that he take first break. He'd relieve her at three a.m., they'd decided, and then he'd be back here by six when the cottage occupants woke up.

He needed to sleep now.

Hubert snored softly beside him, and Elspeth wuffled and moaned. That wasn't disturbing Grady. Grady could sleep in a force-ten gale. He'd done it often.

He'd never done it while thinking of Morag.

The sight of her today had knocked him sideways.

He'd known she was here. Always in the back of his mind he'd known Morag was on Petrel Island. For a while he'd toyed with the idea of staying in contact, but…

But it was an exercise in futility. Morag was beautiful and intelligent and funny and she was fully, absolutely committed.

And it wasn't just commitment to her nephew. It was the commitment to a community that he found so incomprehensible. For Grady, whose life had been spent moving from parent to parent as they'd shifted from one dysfunctional marriage to another, the idea of ties was abhorrent. Ties hurt. His parents had wealth and influence and if there was a problem they paid to have it sorted. They never got involved. He'd learned early that detachment was a way of survival. You showed care and concern when it was appropriate, and then you moved on.

And Morag… She'd excited him four years ago. In Morag he'd recognised the same hunger for excitement. The same ambition. She had been one of the youngest surgical registrars ever to qualify at Sydney Central. She'd thrived on the adrenaline of demanding cases, life-threatening events. When he'd first met her, he'd thought she was gorgeous.

She was still gorgeous.

But she was very different now, he conceded as he stared up at the moonlit ceiling. Her smart little designer suits and jeans, her perfectly shaped curls, they were all things of the past.

In the shock of the news of the tsunami he hadn't thought of Morag. And when he'd seen her…

She'd been wearing ancient jeans that must have been ragged even before the shattering events of the afternoon. She'd worn an oversized man's shirt, and her tangled curls had been bunched back with a piece of crimson ribbon, like a child's. He tried to remember the last time he'd seen her four years ago, the way every curl had known its place. He remembered her sophistication. Her sureness.

She didn't look so much worse now, he conceded. Maybe… maybe even better.

But sophistication? Purpose? Ambition?

Hell, what was he doing, lying in the dark thinking about what a woman looked like? Where a woman was going in life?

Morag…

She was nothing to him, he told himself as he tossed on the hard little bed and tried to force himself into sleep. He needed to sleep. There were still huge medical needs on the island, and the way to operate at less than his best was to allow his mind to wander when it should shut down in sleep.

Morag…

She was just the other side of the wall.

Yeah. In bed with a nine-year-old. Shouldering the responsibilities of a shattered community. Treading a path he knew they could never share.

But…

The briefing he'd had before leaving played over in his head. It had been harsh, fast and to the point.

'Petrel Island is a logistical nightmare, even without the tidal

wave,' he'd been told. 'We've offered the locals reimbursement
if they'll resettle on the mainland. It's too early to say but let's
not focus on rebuilding too early. Let's see what happens.'

If Morag could be persuaded to leave the island... If the
community dispersed, there'd be no real choice.

Maybe then...

Maybe he needed to go to sleep.

Finally he succeeded. Finally he fell asleep—but Morag was
in his dreams.

He'd dreamed of Morag before.

But this was the Morag of now. Not the Morag of yesterday.

CHAPTER FIVE

SHE woke with the first glimmer of dawn.

For a moment Morag didn't know where she was. She only knew that she was warm, the first rays of sun were falling across her face and Robbie's small body was curved into hers.

And then another thought. Somewhere close was Grady.

Grady.

The whole nightmare of yesterday was ready to slam back into place, but as reality hit there were two small comforts holding her steady. Or, if she was honest with herself, they weren't small comforts. They were huge comforts.

Robbie was here. Robbie was safe.

And out in the front room was Grady.

Why should that be a comfort?

Grady's life was disaster management. Grady's life had nothing to do with hers. But now that she was in the midst of the worst kind of disaster, at least Grady could be here. For a tiny while.

And then what?

Reality.

Hamish?

Comfort faded. She felt Robbie stir. The sun had just caught the sill and flooded the bed, disturbing them both. Robbie rolled over and found her, his expression changing from one of panic to relief in a moment.

'Morag. You're here.'

'I'm here.' She'd hugged him in the night as she'd replaced Elspeth and climbed into bed beside him, but she was unsure how awake he'd been. He'd hugged her back but he'd hardly woken. Now she saw consciousness return. And with it relief— but also the enormity of what he'd been through the day before.

64

'Morag,' he said again, and buried his small face against her breast and burst into tears.

She held him. It was all she could think of to do. She'd held him like this too often, she thought drearily. There'd been too many times in this small boy's life when fate had slapped him hard. And now there'd be more people he knew, more people he loved, who he wouldn't see again.

Hamish. Please, God, not Hamish.

Thank God Robbie had been up here with her, she thought. Thank God they both had. If they'd been on the flat and she'd been hurt... If he'd had to cope without her...

No. She was here for him and she wasn't going away.

She had to get up. There was so much to do. A priority had to be a trip out the Koori settlement, she thought, but then... There was so much.

But for this minute there could only be Robbie.

There was a tentative knock and Grady was peering around the door as if he didn't want to intrude. He flinched at the sound of Robbie's sobbing.

'I'm sorry.'

'It's OK.' She gave Robbie a hard hug, ran her fingers through his hair, then lifted his tear-drenched face so she could see him. 'Robbie's having the cry that everyone else had last night. Sometimes the only thing to do is cry. Don't you think so, Dr Reece?'

'I surely do.' He smiled and crossed to the bed, then stood looking down at them. It was a weirdly intimate moment, Morag thought, still dazed by sleep. Grady was standing over Hubert's big bed while she and Robbie lay in a huddle of aunt-nephew sogginess and tried to recover their mutual composure.

At least Grady was composed. He was in his yellow overalls. Dressed and ready for the day, he looked cool and competent and...dangerous?

Where had that word come from? Ridiculous.

'Hi,' Grady was saying, holding his hand out to Robbie. 'I'm

Grady Reece. I've heard about you. I'm a friend of your aunt's—a doctor—and I've come to help.'

Robbie sniffed. He sniffed again but Grady's hand was still outstretched and finally he took it.

'Did you come in the helicopter?' Robbie asked, a trifle warily but seemingly willing to be distracted from his misery.

'That's right.'

'You guys in the yellow overalls were the first to arrive. We saw you land through the field glasses.'

'We're the emergency Air-Sea Rescue team.'

'You came to rescue us?'

'It seems,' Grady said, smiling but with a depth of seriousness behind the smile, 'that you've done a fine job rescuing yourselves already.'

'Some people are dead.'

There was only one answer to that, and Grady had the sense to give it. 'Yes.'

Robbie seemed to think about it. He gazed up at Grady but his small body was still curved into Morag's. And here came the question she'd been dreading. 'What about Hamish?'

'Hamish?' Grady looked questioningly at Morag.

'Hamish is Robbie's cousin and his best friend,' Morag told him, feeling more and more unreal. She was lying in bed discussing the outside world with a man above her, for all the world as if she was a patient and he was her doctor. It was completely alien. It was as if somehow she'd been placed in the position where it was someone else who did the caring. Not her.

Which was ridiculous. Ever since she'd returned to the island the weight of the world had rested firmly on her shoulders, and that weight was never lifted. To think that Grady was somehow going to alleviate that burden was a nonsense.

And there was so much to do...

Grady was still talking to Robbie. Taking his concerns seriously. Let him respond to his query about Hamish, she thought dully. She couldn't.

'I don't know who the islanders are yet.' He raised his brows at Morag. 'Do you know anything about Robbie's friend?'

'I didn't see Hamish yesterday,' Morag admitted. 'I know that his parents—Peter and Christine—were injured. They were the couple you evacuated last night.' She turned back to Robbie. 'Peter and Christine had broken limbs that need to be set by experts in Sydney, but we think they should be OK. As for the kids...one of the nurses told me Lucy had scratches down her leg and they were treating her, but I didn't see her and I haven't seen Hamish. But I've been so busy...'

And that was all she could think of to say. It was all there was to say.

Hamish hadn't been brought into the cricket pavilion with his parents or Lucy. And his name—she was sure Hamish had been on the list as a query. She hadn't had a chance to ask questions.

No. She hadn't been brave enough to ask questions, she conceded. And maybe by now he'd been found. Maybe...

She glanced up at Grady and found his face closed. Uh-oh. Did he know something she didn't?

She still wasn't going to ask. Not now. Not with Robbie listening to every word.

How much grief could one child stand?

'Can I go and look for him?' Robbie asked.

'The professionals are looking for everyone,' Grady said gravely. 'We have people searching everywhere, trying to sort out where everyone is. Meanwhile, your friends are gathering down in one of the big tents. I'm about to go down there and I'll check for myself. Give me Hamish's details and I'll let you know.'

Robbie considered and seemed to find that satisfactory, at least in the short term.

'Is that why you're here?' he asked curiously. 'Do you go round the country rescuing people?'

'We do. I'm a doctor. Our team helps the injured.'

'But there's more people looking than just the guys in yellow overalls.'

'We have the army here as well. They'll keep searching until everyone's found.'

'And then what?'

'What do you mean?' Grady asked. Morag might as well not be there. Robbie was intent on inquisition and Grady, it seemed, was accepting being grilled.

'Will you take us all to the mainland 'cos our island's smashed?'

Whew. What a question. How had Robbie figured that one out?

At least one of them was focused, Morag decided. But it wasn't her. She was feeling more and more disorientated. She was still stunned that somehow she'd ended up in Hubert's bed and she was here, holding Robbie, while this man stood above them...

His yellow overalls looked tough and businesslike, his professionalism accentuated even more by the Air-Sea Rescue insignia on his arm. His hair hadn't been combed this morning—it sort of flopped sideways, looking as if it had been raked by his long fingers over and over. His skin was tanned and weathered, and his eyes crinkled down at them, and he made her feel...

Stop it. Oh, for heaven's sake, stop it, she told herself. Of all the times—and of all the places!—for her to feel the stirring of unashamed lust...

It was totally inappropriate. She turned away from him and gazed at Robbie, who was gazing straight at Grady. He'd clearly decided Grady was hero material, worthy of closer inspection.

'Tell me some of the things you've done,' he was demanding. 'I've read about Air-Sea Rescue. That yacht race last year, was that you? When they had to winch all those people out of the water and the waves were sixty feet high and one of them got his ribs all smashed against the side of the boat...'

'It was me,' Grady said, grinning. He sank down on the bed as if he was a familiar relative rather than a man Robbie had never met. 'Well, it wasn't me who got his ribs smashed, but I was the one who winched him up. Robbie, I hope there'll be time in the next few days for me to sit down and tell you everything about me,' he confided. 'But for now…Hubert says you know pretty much exactly what happened on the island yesterday.'

'We watched through field glasses and then Chris's telescope,' Robbie admitted. 'It was awful. Mr Hamm said if he was younger he'd be out there in his boat to get the people who were swept away, but he couldn't go, so we figured that we'd stay up here and just watch the sea and stay close to the bell. We didn't stop watching until dark.'

'I think you were fantastic,' Grady said gravely. 'But the scientists tell us that the danger's over.'

'Another wave won't come?'

'It's a really long shot, Robbie, and we have seismologists checking for earth tremors all the time now. If there's another wave, there'll be heaps of warning.'

Robbie thought about that and nodded. 'I guess it's not much use watching, then.'

'No. But there's other things we need to do.'

'Like what?' He was still very close to Morag.

'Well, your aunt and I are needed at the medical centre. There are people who were hurt yesterday who need your aunt's care. We have three doctors on the island now and we're all needed.'

'Might people still die?' Robbie asked, and Grady looked gravely down at him.

'They might, Robbie, but not if Morag and I can help it. But while Morag and I are working, I wondered whether you and Hubert would do something that would help Air-Sea Rescue enormously.'

Morag was feeling more and more dazed. This was so like being a hospital patient, she thought, lying in bed while the doctor stood over her, telling her the best course of action for her illness.

And maybe it wasn't a bad thing. The events of the day before had left her shattered, and for her to stay in control now—to take on the responsibility for the entire medical mess—was surely too much. She could operate but only in a subservient capacity, she decided. The normally wilful and decisive Morag was more than content to lie here hugging Robbie while Grady took control.

'What do you want us to do?' Robbie asked.

And Morag thought, Yeah, me too. Count me in on that question.

'We have media arriving,' Grady told Robbie, professional to professional, without a trace of patronage. 'There are reporters from all over the world headed here right this minute. Camera crews, photographers, reporters—you name it. Now, we can't let them down near the harbour. It's too great a mess and it's going to upset everyone to have reporters close. So what we thought was that we'd direct them up here. They'll be coming by helicopter so they can land like we did on the plateau behind this place. I'll have someone rostered to direct them here. You and Hubert can give them a first-hand account of what happened—you realise you're the only ones who had a bird's-eye view of the whole thing? You can point out the whole island from here, and they can take long-range photographs.'

'You mean…you want me to stay up here with Mr Hamm?'

'If you would,' Grady said diffidently, still as if he were asking a colleague for help and not a child. 'If you can keep the reporters happy and out of our hair, it would be enormously appreciated.' He lifted a radio from his belt and laid it on the coverlet beside Robbie. Morag blinked. This was a pretty impressive piece of equipment.

'If you listen in on this, you'll hear everything that's going on with the emergency services all over the island,' he told Robbie. 'You'll be able to keep the reporters up to date. We'll keep you informed as to what's happening.' Then he hesitated, as if suddenly unsure. 'Robbie, Hubert's offered to do this for us, but he's very old and his heart's not so good. I'm hoping you can help.'

But Robbie didn't need persuading. He was already pushing back the covers, the horrors of yesterday receding as he lifted the amazing radio to his ear and started fiddling with buttons.

'I'll be able to hear all over the island?'

'All over the island.'

'You don't need me, do you, Morag?'

'No.' Not true. She missed him already. She missed the warmth of his little body against hers. Grady might be able to deflect Robbie's horrors but he couldn't deflect hers.

But it was time to move on.

'I'm going to talk to Mr Hamm,' Robbie said importantly. 'We have to get organised. You go with Dr Reece, Morag. I'll look after everything up here.'

Morag was left alone with Grady. She wanted to get up— she must get up—but she'd gone to bed in knickers and bra. Her clothes were on the far dresser.

She was a bit stuck.

As for Grady... She'd checked him out by now, and dis- covered that he'd already been out. His big black boots were wet. He'd already been down into the village, she thought, and she knew she had to make herself ask the hard questions.

'What's the latest?' she asked, and Grady nodded as though this was the question he'd been expecting.

'Fifteen confirmed dead. Three from the Koori settlement to add to the list from last night and some missing. But in the meantime, there's some good news. We brought in three fish- ermen during the night. They were coming into harbour when the wave struck. Their boat was smashed but they were wearing lifejackets. One has a broken arm. The other two only copped lacerations and shock. We found them floating half a mile out to sea—there was no way they could fight the currents. Luckily the sea's relatively mild at this time of year so we don't have hypothermia to contend with.'

'Lucky us,' she muttered.

'You have been lucky,' Grady said seriously. 'It could have been so much worse. If you hadn't seen—'

'I did see,' she snapped. 'And fifteen of my people are dead. Don't call me lucky. Do you have a list of the dead?'

'I have a list.'

She caught her breath, suddenly remembering the way he'd backed off a little at Robbie's question.

'Is Hamish still on the list as missing?'

'Yes.' He hesitated. 'Hamish is listed as definitely missing. No one's seen him.'

'Oh, no.'

'Morag, I have no more information than that,' he told her. 'But we're still searching.'

'How many are missing?'

'Three now from the Koori settlement. Only Hamish here.' She swallowed.

'OK.' She closed her eyes. Taking a grip. Moving forward. When she opened her eyes again she was in business mode.

'You've been up for a while?'

'I slept for four hours. I don't need more. I've been organising.'

'Finding spare radios?'

'That, too.'

'To keep Robbie happy?'

'He'll be useful.'

'You could easily have sent someone else up here to cope with the press contingent.'

'Hubert and Robbie together are more than capable.' He smiled, that slow lazy smile that had the power to unsettle her world. Then. In the past. A long time ago. Now a smile couldn't unsettle her. A wave had done that pretty decisively already. 'I've done a fast examination of Hubert,' he told her. 'He's pretty solid. What makes him think he's dying?'

'I revoked his fishing licence,' Morag confessed. 'He hit the jetty at full tilt and pushed a full day's catch by the entire fleet into the bottom of the harbour.'

'So he decided he'd die?'

'Why not? Dying's interesting, as long as you can stretch it out a long, long time.' She managed a fleeting smile. 'And today you've made life even more interesting, for both of them. Thank you.'

'It's self-interest,' he confessed. 'I have need of the island doctor.'

Her smile faded. 'Of course. I'm sorry. I should be up.'

'You needed to sleep. There's a lot to cope with, Morag,' he told her seriously. 'As you said, these are your people. We're coping with major trauma—major physical damage— but as well as that there's also shocking emotional damage. If you're strong enough to work through this, you'll be our most valuable medic.'

'You mean…you're being nice to me so that I can cope mentally with what's coming?'

'Something like that.' He smiled down at her, his eyes crinkling at the corners. 'Hey, Morag, it's really good to see you again.'

'It's good to see you, too,' she whispered. He didn't know how much. 'What do you want me to do?'

'Cope. Not collapse. My job is to support you. I can do hands-on physical stuff but this community needs you if it's going to be viable.'

'You're thinking it's still viable?'

'I don't know what the decision will be.'

'I want to be in on that decision-making.' She eyed her clothes on the dresser and thought about making a grab for them. To be sitting in bed…

'Of course you do,' he agreed. 'And one of my tasks is to make sure you're capable of that.' He smiled again. 'Now, I'm going to make us some toast. Do you want some space to get dressed or do you want some help?'

Help her with dressing? He had to be kidding. 'I can cope.'

'I'm sure you can.' His smile faded. 'You seem to have coped so far. Alone.'

'I haven't had much choice.'

'No.'

Silence. It was a tangible thing, this silence. It was loaded with history and with pain.

Loaded with emptiness.

'Get dressed, love,' he said at last, almost roughly. 'I'll make you breakfast, but we need to move fast. For today we need each other.' Then he grinned and reached for her pile of clothes. 'Here's your modesty. You know, you really do remind me of you.'

They both knew what he meant by that. Once upon a time he'd thought he'd fallen in love.

With someone who was no longer her.

CHAPTER SIX

SHE might fleetingly remind Grady of the Morag she'd once been, she thought bitterly as the morning progressed, but the old Morag was long gone. The sophisticated career-woman who'd only cared for herself... Ha!

Even that thought hardly had time to surface. Everywhere Morag looked there was need. Aching, tearing need that she had no hope of meeting. The walk back down to the ruined township had her stopping time and time again as people wept on her, people hugged her, people tried to talk through their fears.

But at least she wasn't the town's only doctor. At least she had help. They all had help.

It seemed the Petrel Island tsunami had caught the sympathy of the world, and resources were pouring in. Huge Chinook helicopters were ferrying in resources as fast as they could, and already there was order emerging from the catastrophe.

Last night the cricket ground had looked like a massive disaster area. Now huge tents held dormitory-style bunks for everyone. Apparently even those whose homes were undamaged were being advised to stay here. The huge wash of water had caused more than direct problems, with landslips and flooding leading to sewerage and plumbing nightmares.

But engineering problems, thankfully, weren't Morag's worry. She had enough to face without that.

The place Grady took Morag to—finally—was another huge white tent. It turned out to be a stunningly set-up field hospital.

People had worked all through the night, Morag realised, dazed and washed with guilt that she'd slept through such an effort.

'You needed to sleep,' Grady said gently as they stood at

75

the entrance to the big tent. Damn, how could he guess what she was thinking almost before she knew she was thinking it? 'You were so shocked and exhausted that you were past operating. Do you want to see Sam?'

'He's not been evacuated?'

'We're taking him out this morning.' He grimaced. 'There was the small matter of his cat.'

'Sam's cat.' Morag thought about Sam's cat while she stared around her.

The tent had a foyer, just like a real hospital. A woman clad in emergency-services yellow was seated at a desk, directing traffic. Two corridors led off—one labelled EMERGENCY and the other WARDS. Wards? How could they have done this in such a short space of time?

It looked unreal. If it hadn't been for the grass underfoot, the building could have been a city clinic.

Her head was spinning. She had to focus on one thing at a time. Hamish. The Kooris.

Sam's cat. That was easiest.

'I know Oscar,' she said. The vast, overfed tom was almost an institution on the island. He was fiercely protective of his master, and most of the islanders actively disliked him. He hissed and spat at anyone who came near Sam's boat. If anyone threatened his Sam—and that might be by saying hello and holding out a hand to be shaken—then Oscar knew what to do. He ruled the island cats with well-sharpened claws, and he wore each of his many battle scars like the tattoos on the toughest of bikie gangsters.

'He would have been on the boat with Sam,' Morag said, dismayed. Oscar was definitely not her favourite cat, but she knew how heartbroken Sam would be without him.

'That's right,' Grady told her, smiling. 'He was washed out of the boat with Sam, and Sam's wife assumed he was dead. But Sam wasn't having a bar of it and insisted on staying until he found out. Anyway, about an hour ago Heather came marching into the hospital with the most bedraggled cat you've ever seen. She dumped it on Sam's coverlet and said, ''Here, here's your damned cat, now you can get yourself fixed up properly.'' The cat's fine. Elsey, our chief nurse, tried to be nice and approached Oscar with a towel. Oscar put two fang marks in her hand and she'll have to have a course of antibiotics. Despite losing his leg, suddenly all's almost OK with Sam's world.'

Grady was smiling. And suddenly so was Morag.

This was normal. These were her people, responding as they must to extraordinary circumstances. For the first time she thought there might be a tomorrow.

And this was the worst. From here, it could only move forward.

'What do you want me to do about it?' she asked.

'Explain to Sam why he can't take his cat to the mainland?'

'I can do that.'

'Find someone to offer to look after it?'

'Harder,' she admitted. 'But Oscar hangs around the lighthouse. I can put cat food out. Not that he'll deign to eat it. He steals food from every kitchen in the island. Then what?'

His smile faded. 'Morag...' He hesitated but she knew as soon as he looked at her—as soon as his smile faded—what he was going to ask.

'Morag, the injuries we've got are substantial. The worst have been evacuated but we've got twenty beds filled. Sadly, the injured people are mostly those who were in the worst places, and because it was a Sunday they tended to be in family groups. So we have injured people where there's often a matching death. We'll bring in trained counsellors, but these people need to talk straight away and you're their family doctor. We've decided that unless there's further immediate trauma, your most urgent need is to check the lists, get yourself up to speed, then go from bed to bed and talk people through what's happened. As you have been on the way here. These people need you, Morag, and that need is more for talk than for action.'

She nodded. She'd expected no less.

It was odd, she thought dully. Four years ago she'd wanted desperately to be a surgeon. She hadn't wanted one bit of personal medicine. The sooner patients were anaesthetised and she could concentrate on technical skills rather than interpersonal stuff, the better she'd liked it.

But now... Interpersonal stuff was medicine just as surely as surgery. She knew what Grady was asking was just as necessary as hands-on trauma stuff, and every bit as important. Maybe even more so.

'Check injuries yourself as you go,' Grady was saying. 'Yesterday was chaos. Look for things that may have been missed. There are still people coming in. My team and I can cope with front-line stuff, but you need to do the personal. Can you do that?'

'Of course I can.'

'Good.' He hesitated and then shook his head. 'No. I'm sorry. Of course it's not good. But it's what you're here for, Morag. Four years ago it was your decision to be a part of this. For now I'm afraid you have to live with it.'

She did. And maybe she needed to start thinking for herself. 'I need to go out to the Koori settlement before I do anything else,' she told him. 'They'll need me.'

'Jaqui's gone out there now.'

She frowned. That was a waste. If they'd asked her... 'They won't let her help.'

'Why not?'

'They hardly let me.'

'She'll be able to give us an overview at least,' Grady told her. 'Surely. But you're needed here. With only three doctors I can't afford for you both to be there, and she's already gone. She's good, Morag. I think you'll find she can help. You work here for this morning and if there's a need you can go out there yourself this afternoon.'

'There will be a need.'

'There's need here, Morag. There's need everywhere.'

'Grady, I need to prioritise. The Kooris—'

But Angie Salmon had been standing in the shadows, waiting for them to finish. As Morag caught her eye, the woman stepped forward. She looked distraught to the point of despair.

'Morag,' she faltered. 'I just wanted… I just… I didn't sleep and the kids are hysterical and Don's blaming himself and all he can do is cry and… I need…'

Priorities. How could she choose?

She just had to trust that Jaqui could pull off a miracle out in the Koori settlement.

She had to trust in Grady.

So for the rest of the morning she moved from one personal tragedy to the next. Listening.

She listened to Angie, then tucked her firmly into bed and gave her something to make her sleep. 'You're no use to anyone if you collapse,' she told her. 'Get yourself strong. Others are looking after your kids. I'll see Don and we'll work something out so you can both have time out.'

It was no solution—there *was* no solution—but it was all she could do.

Grady and his team worked a surgery, assessing, treating, assigning beds, organising evacuations. The rest was left to Morag. It was too much for one doctor to handle, but she was the only one who could do it.

And it was mind-numbing work. Dreadful. They didn't teach you this at medical school, Morag thought as she cradled old Hazel Cartwright against her breast and listened to her sobs. Elias Cartwright had been slightly demented and hugely demanding. When the wave had hit, Hazel had been out walking, taking a breather from her heavy role of carer. The wave had killed Elias instantly. Even though Hazel had expected her husband's death any time these past ten years, shock had her in a grief as deep as that felt by Angie.

There was little Morag could do but listen to Hazel. There was little she could do for anyone but listen.

Over and over she heard the stories. Where people had been.

How they'd felt as the wave had hit. How they couldn't do anything. The feeling of sheer absolute helplessness, of lives suddenly out of control in the face of this catastrophe.

That was the deepest feeling. Being out of control.

Like Hazel… Death in bed at the end of a long life, death by misadventure, even death by disease—these things could be explained. Somehow. But to have the island decimated like this…to lose faith in their very foundations…

All Morag could do was listen.

But sometimes there were practicalities. Sometimes there was pain she could alleviate.

Like thirteen-year-old Lucy, huddled in bed, miserable and alone and frantically fearful because both her parents had been airlifted to Sydney and her brother was missing. She'd been treated for gravel rash—she'd been swept along a road in the same motion as being dumped by a wave, only this time the beach had been the gravel road outside her home. Her parents had been badly injured, and Lucy had been the one to run for help, so her injuries had been only cursorily inspected by one of the nurses in the first hours when Morag had been so occupied. She needed to be reassessed now.

She didn't want to be reassessed. Morag reached her bed and the teenager's face closed, almost in anger. But as she turned away from Morag, she winced.

The gravel rash was on her left. She'd turned to her right. What was wrong with her right side?

Morag put her hand on the girl's left shoulder and let it lie. Softly. As if she had all the time in the world.

'Your arm's hurting?'

'No.'

'I think it is.'

'Everything hurts.'

They should have evacuated Lucy as well, Morag thought, but even if she had gone to Sydney, her parents were in no condition to comfort her. And someone had thought, What if Hamish was found, injured?

But it wasn't fair on Lucy. She should be with her parents.

'Where's your grandmother?' she asked. May wasn't on any list. Was the sprightly elderly lady out looking for her grandson?

'She came in before,' Lucy muttered. 'I told her to go away.'

'To look for Hamish?'

'Hamish is dead.'

'We don't know that.'

'Yeah, we do,' Lucy spat. 'Where else would he be?'

Morag closed her eyes. Deep breath.

'Your grandma will need you as much as you need her,' she said, but had a fierce head-shake in return.

'I don't want anyone.'

'Lucy?'

'What?'

'Let me see your arm.'

'My arm doesn't matter. I want to know what's happened to my parents.'

Before she saw each patient, Morag did her homework, finding out as much as she could about what had happened to each of their families and discovering, if she could, the extent of the damage to their homes. She'd treated Peter and Christine last night and she'd read the report on the family house. Plus, she'd checked. So now she was able to give as much reassurance as there was to give.

'I radioed Sydney fifteen minutes ago,' she told her. 'Your dad has a fractured thigh and the doctors in Sydney are operating on him right now. Your mum hurt one of her legs as well. It's a simple fracture that only needs a plaster, but she also hit her head. That's why she was drifting in and out of consciousness when you last saw her. But she's conscious now. The Sydney doctors will be doing all sorts of tests in Sydney and we'll tell you the minute we know.'

'What are they testing for?'

'For insurance,' a man's voice said behind Morag, and it was Grady.

Grady.

Morag had been working solidly for about four hours. She hadn't realised how exhausted she was, but when she turned and saw him she felt the pressure lift—just like that. He was dressed in a green theatre gown, with his mask pushed down as if he'd just emerged from surgery. She'd guess that he'd been working as hard as she had, if not harder.

So there was no reason for her to look to him for support. Was there? But as he pushed aside the curtain dividing Lucy's bed from the rest of the tent, it was all she could do not to stand up and hug him.

He saw it. He gave her a small, reassuring smile, which should have been nothing but it gave her the strength to take another deep breath and carry on.

Grady's smile had moved to Lucy. Good. The girl needed more reassurance than Morag could give.

'I was the one who assessed your mother before she left,' Grady was telling her. 'She was drifting in and out of consciousness then, but I think shock might have been having an effect, as well as the pain from her broken leg. There didn't seem to be any intracranial swelling.'

'Intracranial swelling?'

'Sometimes when people hit their heads they bleed into their brains,' Grady told the girl. 'Pressure can cause major problems. But usually when that happens you can tell. You open people's eyes and check their pupils. I checked your mum's eyes and her pupils looked fine.'

'What would they look like if they weren't fine?' Lucy demanded, almost belligerently.

'When you shine a light in people's eyes, a normal, undamaged brain makes the pupils get smaller,' Grady told her. 'I shone a light into your mother's eyes and her pupils reacted just as they should. Also, her pupils stayed exactly the same as each other. That's a really good sign.'

'So why did you send her to Sydney?'

'Just as a precaution,' Grady told her. 'So if things change or if I was wrong and she does need an operation to relieve pressure, then she'll be in the right spot. And your dad was going anyway.'

'Why couldn't I go?'

'No room on the helicopter,' Grady told her bluntly.

Lucy hesitated. 'What about Hamish?'

'We're still looking for Hamish.'

Lucy hesitated. Her face closed in what almost seemed teenage rebellion. 'I don't want to stay on this island any more,' she whispered. The teenager's eyes were determinedly defiant, but there was more than a hint of moisture behind them now. It was as much as Morag could do not to gather her in for a hug—but she knew instinctively that it wouldn't help. It was a fine line—when a kid turned into an adolescent and when a hug from an adult became patronising and claustrophobic.

It was only for a few short years that teenagers became untouchable and it was dreadful that this had happened right in the midst of it. But if it got worse…

Grady flicked a questioning look at Morag, colleague asking permission, and he got an imperceptible nod in return. It was fine by Morag. This was no time for being precious about patient boundaries. She wanted all the help she could get.

'If Dr Morag is worried about your arm, maybe we could look at it together,' Grady suggested.

'My arm's OK.'

'There's no medals for heroes in this game,' Grady said gently. 'Lucy, I've been treating grown men this morning with lesser injuries than you, and some of them have been crying. You don't need to pretend, and no one will tell anyone if you have a really good howl. Now…let us look at your arm.'

Lucy stared at Grady for a long moment. Grady gazed calmly back.

And Lucy cracked first.

'OK,' she conceded.

'Sensible decision,' Grady told her, without a flicker of relief that the girl had agreed.

Then, as Morag watched from the sidelines, he sat on the bed and carefully lifted Lucy's arm.

'Can you move your fingers?'

'Yeah.'

'Try.'

He got a belligerent look, but he met Lucy's gaze calmly and dispassionately. He was a fine doctor, Morag thought. He had so many skills. But, then, she'd known that about him all along.

'Who's looking for Hamish?' she whispered, and Grady met that with calmness as well.

'We have every fit islander, plus a team of almost fifty army personnel, combing the island.'

'He was swept away with the wave?'

'I guess he must have been,' Grady told her, feeling each finger and watching her face. 'The wave hit you and your parents with such force—'

'But Hamish wasn't with us.'

Morag stilled. The search for the small boy—for Robbie's best mate—was centring around the fact that he'd been swept out from his parents' front yard. His parents had been too dazed to do any more than ask for news of their son, and Lucy hadn't been questioned. The searchers were working in the assumption that he'd been with his parents when the wave had struck.

Dangerous assumption. She saw Grady focus, and his hand came out to take the girl's good one.

'Lucy, we've been searching for Hamish around your house. Are you saying he could be somewhere else on the island?'

'He went over to Morag's.'

'To the lighthouse?' Morag's heart sank. The promontory that held the lighthouse had been swept clean by the force of the wave. If Hamish had been out there... 'Did he come over to see Robbie?'

'Yeah. Mum said he should do his school project but Dad said he it was too good a day to keep a kid inside.' Her face crumpled and she gave a despairing whimper. 'It's not fair. He shouldn't have gone. Where is he? I want my mum.'

'I tell you what we'll do,' Grady told her, as, like it or not, Morag moved to hug the girl close. Lucy was so distressed that she suddenly almost seemed to welcome it, her body curving into Morag's like she belonged there. Only for a moment. Only for a second. Then she regrouped and pulled away. But somehow…her hand stayed just within contact with Morag's.

'We'll X-ray your arm. If, as I think, you've fractured your forearm, we'll put it into plaster so it doesn't move and it stops hurting,' Grady told her. 'And then we'll organise a helicopter flight for you to the mainland so you can be with your dad while you wait for your mother to get better.'

'But Hamish…'

'We're doing all we can, Lucy.'

'Can I ask your Grandma to come in?' Morag asked, and the girl's face closed again.

'No,' she muttered. 'I don't want to see her again. Grandma started crying. Grandma never cries. I don't know what to tell her. Hamish…'

'Can you remember,' Morag said carefully, trying to make it sound as if it was important but not too important, 'how long it was between Hamish leaving home and the wave hitting?'

'He left home just after lunch and we have lunch at one,' Lucy said fretfully. 'I remember 'cos Dad said he couldn't go until we'd done the washing-up.'

'We left the lighthouse just before two,' Morag told Grady. 'He must have just missed us.'

'Mum said if Robbie wasn't home he had to come straight back,' Lucy told them. 'He had loads of homework to do. It was Dad's idea to let him go but I think Mum was a bit pissed off.'

'Where else would Hamish have gone?' Grady asked her. 'If Robbie wasn't home, were there any other friends he'd contact?'

'I don't know.' The teenager seemed to realise Morag was

still in contact with her hand, and she pulled back some more, whimpering a little as her arm jarred. She hauled up her bed-covers as if they could protect her from impending pain. 'I don't know.'

'We'll look,' Morag promised, but she couldn't promise that they'd find him.

They knew the odds.

The odds were dreadful.

Lucy's arm had a simple greenstick fracture. Morag assisted while Grady carefully prepped the arm, wrapped it and then put a backslab on the forearm. There was considerable swelling around the wrist. Given that it had happened over twelve hours ago, it was probably as swollen as it was going to be. It'd have to be checked in a few days.

In a few days Lucy would be in Sydney, Morag thought. Hopefully with her recovering mother and father.

And her brother?

The impending tragedy stayed with them while they worked. Lucy was white-faced and silent, and they knew her silence wasn't caused by her own pain. She was terrified for her parents and for her brother—and she had every right to be.

'I'll contact Sydney,' Grady said, grim-faced, as they left Lucy with a nurse and came out again into the little reception area. 'Maybe the father might know where Hamish might be?'

'I'll contact him,' Morag told him. 'Peter's my friend.' She grimaced. 'And Christine is Robbie's aunt. Christine's brother was Beth's husband—Robbie's father. He drowned when Robbie was tiny, so they know already what tragedy is.'

That hurt. 'Oh, hell…'

'It is,' she said bleakly. 'Hamish is Robbie's cousin and they've been extraordinarily close all their lives. If I hadn't come back when I did, Robbie would be part of their family.'

'They would have taken him in?'

'Of course.'

He frowned. 'So why did you come back?'

Why had she come back? Did he understand nothing?

'That's a great question,' she snapped. 'Very empathetic. Look around you at this community and use your head. Is Jaqui back from the Koori settlement?'

'She's been back for a while.'

Morag stilled. 'So they didn't let her help.'

'I gather not. They said there were no problems.'

'Oh, sure. No problems? They'd hide them.'

'Why would they hide them?'

'They just would.' She raked her hair in distress. 'I should have gone.' None of the Koori people would admit to Jaqui that they needed help, she thought grimly. She'd been stupid to hope that they would.

'If Jaqui can't help, how can you?' Grady asked.

'They trust me.'

'But—'

'There's no but,' she snapped. 'Of course they won't let Jaqui near them. I should have been out there this morning. Or last night! It's taken my family two generations to get their trust, and I have it. So I'm needed. Ask me again why I came home, Dr Reece.'

'I never meant—'

'I know you never meant,' she said softly, almost under her breath. 'You never meant anything.'

First she had to make the phone call to Peter—Hamish's father—and it was dreadful. For this little family, the drowning of Beth's husband—Christine's brother—followed by Beth's death, was still real and dreadful, and Morag could hear the horror of past pain as well as terror for the future in the way Peter spoke to her. Peter was badly injured himself, just coming around from anaesthesia. His wife was still not out of danger. And...where was his son?

'I was sure he'd be with Robbie,' he told her. 'I was sure. When they said he was still missing... I just said find Robbie and he'll be there. They said Robbie was up with Hubert so I just assumed…' His voice broke. 'I can't believe I left the island not knowing. I was just so worried about Christine. And I couldn't find May.'

May was Peter's mother. At least she could reassure him there. 'I've seen May and she's OK. She's worried to death about Hamish, of course, but she was out of range when the wave hit and her house is undamaged.' She was worried to death about Lucy as well, but Lucy still wouldn't let her close and she wasn't about to burden Peter with his mother's distress. 'She'll be here for Hamish when we find him. And you were so badly hurt yourself,' Morag said gently. 'Peter, we're doing all we can.'

'He must have followed you up to Hubert's.' Peter's voice cracked with desperation. 'Maybe he'd guess that you'd be up there. Maybe…'

'I'll check everything,' Morag told him. 'Meanwhile, we're sending Lucy over to be with you.'

'But if Hamish needs her… If May needs her…'

'I'll be here for Hamish and for May, I promise.'

Distressed beyond measure, she put the phone down and turned to find Grady watching her. His face was etched deep with concern.

'Dreadful?'

'Dreadful,' she agreed. 'That little family's lost so much already. I'm worried Peter might crack up completely.'

'He can't,' Grady said bluntly. 'His wife and daughter depend on him.'

'Yeah.' She shrugged, still cringing inside from the pain she'd heard in Peter's voice. 'It does hold you up. This feeling that if you fall over it'll have a domino effect.' She took a deep breath. 'Maybe I need to speak to Robbie. He and Hamish were planning to spend the afternoon together before Hamish's mum said he had to spend the afternoon on homework. I wonder what were they planning to do?'

'Homework together?' Grady queried, and she managed a smile.

'Or not.' Her smile faded. 'I need to phone Robbie before I go out to the settlement.'

'I've cleared the way to come with you.'

'You don't want—'

'I need. As you say, there may well be medical imperatives out there. If I'm assisting you, will that be OK?'

'Maybe. If you're seen as the junior partner with no authority.' Her worry receded for a whole split second while she thought of the impossibility of Grady being the junior partner in anything.

'I'll be the junior partner,' he said, with a meekness that had her glancing at him with suspicion, but his face was impassive. 'Phone Robbie. I'll start loading gear.'

Robbie knew nothing.

'I dunno where he'd be.' Robbie had held up so well, but the thought of losing Hamish had him almost incoherent with anguish. 'We were just going to do…stuff.'

'What sort of stuff?'

'I dunno.' There was an audible sniff on the end of the line. 'Morag, can you come and get me? Now?'

'I need to go out to the aboriginal settlement,' she told him, almost twisting inside with pain. He needed her. He needed her so much, but she was stuck. To take her with him when she didn't know what she'd find…she couldn't. But she had to go.

He had to see it.

'Robbie, the Koori people…many of them may well be hurt and they won't let anyone near except me.'

He gulped and she heard him fight back tears. 'Do you…do you want me to stay another night with Hubert?'

'If you can, Robbie,' she said gently. 'I know it's a lot to ask, but so many people here need me. I'll come up later and share Hubert's bed again.'

Then she was forced to listen while he fought panic. But finally he managed to do the right thing. The adult thing. The thing that a nine-year-old shouldn't have to do when he was faced with what Robbie had faced in the past, and what he was facing in the future.

'I'll be OK,' he quavered.

'You're a good kid, Robbie.'

'Sometimes I get sick of being a good kid,' he said rebelliously, and she winced.

'You know something, Robbie?'

'What?'

'Sometimes I get sick of being a good adult, too,' she confessed. 'You reckon one day you and I might run away from home?'

He thought about it, but only for a moment.

'If they close down the island, we won't have to run away. They'll chuck us off.'

'There could be a good side to that. Maybe we wouldn't have to be good any more.'

'Yeah, but you'd just get a job somewhere else and we'd have to be good all over again,' he told her. 'We'd better stay here.'

'OK.'

'But, Morag…'

'Mmm?'

'I'll stay here and be good,' he told her. 'But you find Hamish.'

CHAPTER SEVEN

'ROBBIE'S taking it hard?'

Grady hadn't said a word until they had one of the few undamaged four-wheel-drives loaded and were headed south toward the Koori settlement. He produced sandwiches and handed them to her piece by piece as she drove. She knew the way and it seemed suddenly important that she keep the illusion that she was in control. But Grady was glancing across at her as she drove, and she knew that he saw that her knuckles were white on the steering-wheel.

And one sandwich seemed enough to choke her.

'Morag?' he prodded gently, and she had to force herself to respond.

What had he asked? Was Robbie taking it hard? Stupid, stupid question.

'You don't know how much.'

'You've really dug yourself deep here, haven't you?'

'No,' she said tightly. 'I haven't dug myself anywhere. The hole's been dug for me.'

'You elected to come.'

'Yeah,' she said tightly. 'I did.'

'Were you happy here?' he asked. 'Before the wave struck.'

'Of course I was happy. Why wouldn't I be happy?'

'You don't miss Sydney?'

Oh, for heaven's sake. What a time for an inquisition.

'Why should I miss Sydney?' she snapped.

'I just thought—'

'Well, don't think.' She hesitated. And then thought, No, why not say it? All these things that had built up for so long…

'Why would I ever want to be somewhere other than here?' she told him, her anger suddenly threatening almost to overwhelm her. 'I like there being only three shops on the island. I like always drinking instant coffee and wearing the same clothes everyone else wears, and I like it that everyone on the island knows every single thing about my life. I like having dated the island's only two eligible men—and deciding they weren't so eligible after all. I like cooking our own dinner every damned night except once a month when Robbie and I treat ourselves to dinner at the pub where we have a choice of steak and chips, fish and chips or sausages and chips. I like being on call twenty-four hours a day, seven days a week and fifty-two weeks of the year. And I like it that Robbie will have to go to Sydney to board for the last few years of secondary school and he'll probably never come back and I'll be stuck here for ever…'

Her voice broke and she dashed an angry hand across her face. Tears? When had she last cried? Before yesterday, she couldn't remember.

'So if the island is declared unfit for habitation,' Grady said cautiously into the stillness, 'you won't be too upset?'

She swivelled. They hit a bump on the dirt track and the truck lurched, but she didn't notice.

'What the hell are you talking about?'

'The infrastructure's been smashed. It'll cost a bomb to fix the power and sewerage and the buildings. It'd be much cheaper for the government to pay for resettlement on the mainland.'

'Oh, great.'

'You don't want to be here.'

'I didn't say that.'

'I think you just did.'

'Well, I didn't!' She was so angry now she was almost spitting. 'I know. I miss things from the mainland. Of course I do. And I feel trapped. But these people… A tiny group of highlanders settled here two hundred years ago and their descendants still live here. Most of the kids now leave the island when they're about fourteen to go to secondary school and a lot of them don't come back. But the ones that do…they come because they want to.'

'Maybe they feel obligated. Like you.'

'So you'd say let's not give them the choice?'

'If it costs a bomb…maybe not.'

'And the true islanders?' she snapped. 'The Koori? They've been here for thousands of years. They keep apart from the rest of the island. They speak their own language. They're the most extraordinary artists and craftsmen. Magical. But their way of life hasn't changed in generations. Except that they get emergency health care and inoculations.'

'Thanks to you, and you don't want to be here.'

'I didn't say that.'

'You did.'

'No,' she snapped. 'I said I missed things. I do. Of course I do. But if I truly wanted to leave, you wouldn't see me for dust.'

'And if you and I…'

'What?' She turned and faced him and the truck hit a stump in the road. The truck jerked sideways and she swore and pulled the car to a halt. Maybe driving when she was white hot with rage wasn't such a good idea.

'There's still something between us, Morag,' Grady told her. He was watching her face. Carefully. Choosing his words. 'You know, I haven't forgotten you. All these years… If you came back…'

It needed only that.

'You're saying we could take up where we left off four years ago?'

'I didn't realise how much I'd miss you,' he said softly. 'Until you left.'

She closed her eyes. After all these years. At such a time…

'I'm sorry,' he said gently. 'This isn't the time.'

'No.' Her eyes flew wide and she stared straight ahead at the road. Carefully she steered back from the verge, keeping careful rein on her fury. 'No, it's not.' Then, very carefully, thinking it through, she said, 'Grady, when you came here, were you told to start preparing us for full evacuation?'

'I—'

'I know it's early,' she said. 'The focus is on searching. But there's a huge number of troops on the island now, yet the main road's still blocked. And I was talking to one of the men who's been working on the gas main. He was telling me that they'd succeeded in blocking it completely. Now, that might just be temporary, for safety…'

'It is.'

'So you know that for sure?' she said carefully. 'You seem to be taking care of me, but people are deferring to you. You're some sort of leader in all this. Can you tell me for sure that there are no plans to declare this island unfit for habitation?'

She waited. She kept driving.

There was no answer from beside her.

She'd expected none.

'I'm right, aren't I?' she said grimly. 'Well, it's not going to happen. We won't all leave.'

'If there are no services…'

'If there's no services, most of the townspeople will leave,' she told him. 'Of course they will. They have no choice. Even the people like Hubert. I dare say if you removed his pension and took away all support, then maybe he'd be forced to go, too. But not the Kooris.'

'Do the Koori need our intervention?'

'No,' she snapped. 'Of course they don't. They don't want us helping in any way, shape or form. They'll tell you that over and over. So do you believe them? You'd leave them to fend for themselves.'

'If that's what they want.'

'You don't know anything about what they want,' she said dully. 'You know nothing at all. Just shut up, Grady. Help me if you can, but shut up about the future. I need to focus on putting one foot in front of the other and that's all I want to do. And as for you and me… Ha!'

*   *   *

He said nothing.

It was like he was stepping on eggshells, he thought. Try as he may, he was about to crush things he had no wish to crush.

And he wasn't at all sure what it was he was crushing.

He didn't understand. He knew nothing. That was what she'd accused him of, and she was right. He had no understanding of this small community, of the dynamics that held it together and why its hold on Morag was so strong.

And behind everything... The thought nagged.

There'd been an alternative for Robbie. Robbie had an Uncle Peter and an Aunt Christine and a cousin Lucy, and maybe even still a cousin Hamish. Four years ago Morag had implied there was no one for the boy. That was why he'd let her go.

No. No one let Morag go anywhere, he thought as he watched her heave her gear from the back of the truck and turn to welcome the two old Koori men who'd appeared to greet her as the truck had drawn to a halt. She was her own woman. She did what she wanted.

She hadn't wanted him.

Of course she had, he told himself. She'd wanted him as much as he'd wanted her, but she'd wanted this community more. And it wasn't just her wishes that were holding her here. She was tied by the community's needs.

For Grady, who'd been raised with immense wealth but with no commitment to anyone, this was a concept he found almost impossible to comprehend. Commitment to people. Love, not for just one person but for five hundred...

Hell. He was too confused to think this through any further. All he could do was watch.

The cove where they'd parked the truck was as far from the township as it was possible to be. There were no visible buildings. A band of palms surrounded a broad sweep of beach. Wide strips of rock ribboned the sides of the cove, and even from two hundred yards away he could see white crusting that spoke of generation upon generation of oysters, building on the remains of their past.

The cove itself... It must have been beautiful yesterday, he thought, but the wave had ripped it apart. Some of the smaller palms had been uprooted and a mass of mud, leaf litter and assorted debris coated everything. In the shadows of the palms he could make out the flitting figures of dark-skinned people, fading back behind the trees as if scared of these people appearing from another world.

Morag was ignoring him. She was speaking to the two men, urgently, in a dialect he didn't recognise. Their language? It must be.

The men were elderly, white-haired, with deep, brown skin that was covered only between their waist and their knees. One of the men had a jagged wound running down the side of his shoulder. He put a hand to it occasionally, as if it hurt.

Morag looked as if she hadn't noticed.

They spoke for a good five minutes, the old men softly spoken but obviously hugely distressed. As they spoke they paused every so often to glance across at him with a look that said they were deeply distrustful.

Distrustful. Great. He tried very hard to merge into the pile of medical supplies and look harmless.

How did you look harmless?

But finally they broke apart, and Morag led the men across to where Grady stood.

'Dr Reece, this is Yndilla and Nargal. Yndilla, Nargal, this is Dr Reece.' She was speaking slowly, giving the men time to understand a language they were clearly not comfortable with. 'We want to start work now,' she told the men. 'Will you bring us those you believe we can help?' She hesitated. 'But, please...remember that wounds from coral or oyster shells get infected fast, and remember that we can help stop that infection.' Then, as their expressions again became uncertain, she reverted again to their language.

Once again, Grady could do nothing but wait.

Finally the two white heads inclined ever so slightly. It seemed permission had been given.

'What's happening?' Grady asked, as the men disappeared into the shadows to talk to their people.

'They've lost seven of their own,' she told him, gazing after the elders with a worried look. 'A lot of the kids ran to the beach when the water was sucked out, and they were hit hard. But most of them survived. These people live in the water. They knew enough to let themselves be washed out and then swim in after the first rush. The deaths will have been caused by injury. Two elderly men. One woman, two babies and two little girls.'

He winced. And then he moved to organisational mode. This was, after all, work he was trained for. 'OK. We need to transport the bodies to town. Can I call someone?'

She shook her head. 'They're already buried.'

'But the coroner—'

'The coroner accepts the judgment of the tribe elders,' she told him. 'So do I. Yndilla and Nargal have agreed to let us see the urgent medical cases, and for that I'm grateful.'

'Yndilla has a gash that needs stitching.'

'No.' Once more she shook her head. 'He won't let us stitch it. He says he hit it on a rock, and he's cleaned it.'

'It'll scar.'

She smiled. 'Yeah. Right. Did you see his chest?'

He had. The old man's chest was crossed with scars that were obviously part of some tribal ritual, and there was no doubt that the scars were worn with pride. A slash across the old man's shoulder was hardly likely to have him cringe with self-consciousness.

She was still smiling and the corners of his mouth curved involuntarily in response. He liked it when she smiled, he thought. He…

He nothing.

Hell. Back to work.

'What else?'

'There's a couple of suspected fractures that probably need setting,' she told him. 'Kids. We're permitted to give pain relief while we set them.'

'But X-rays...'

'No X-rays unless there's a real call for it.'

'Like if we think it's broken?'

'No. These people live rough. There are fractures all the time. They won't tolerate me taking kids into hospital for a greenstick fracture.'

He stared. 'Hell, Morag...'

'We do what we can,' she said simply. Then she shrugged. 'I know you don't like it but it's the way it is. If there's a major problem, if it's clear that a leg's going to end up shorter than the other or not heal at all, then I'll push hard, and because they know I don't push unless it's imperative, usually they'll agree. But it needs huge persuasion, Grady, so I don't try unless I think it's really, really dire.' She hesitated, giving him a searching glance. 'So...can you start on the fractures? The elders will stay with you all the time. They have a little English if you speak slowly, and they'll translate as best they can.'

'And you?'

'There's an old lady I need to see. She's with the women.' She hesitated. 'Just don't ask me about her, Grady. Can I leave you to the rest?'

'Sure.'

'Right.' But still she hesitated. 'Grady...please, remember that these people don't want intervention. No dressings unless they're really necessary. Same with stitches. Stitches get infected. Scars will become part of the legend of this tsunami. They'll be shown with pride to grandchildren. So we're not interested in cosmetic results, right?'

'Right.'

'Fine,' she said, and cast him an uncertain smile. Then a woman called out from the shadows. Morag hesitated, but there was nothing left to say. She was being forced to trust him, he thought, watching her face, and he knew that it was a weird sensation.

He watched in silence as she collected her doctor's bag and strode into a mass of palms at the back of the clearing. Leaving him with the shadows fading in and out of the cover of the palms.

Leaving him…confused.

There wasn't time for confusion, however. He had things to do.

Nargal emerged first from the backdrop of palms. The old man had a child by his side, a little girl of about six or seven. She was holding one arm with the other, and was big-eyed with pain and fear.

Nargal looked almost as terrified.

Morag had persuaded these people to trust him, he thought, and suddenly the responsibility of what he was facing seemed enormous. One bad move and these people would disappear into their shadows, he knew, and then…and then there'd only be Morag who'd be allowed near.

She was desperately alone. This was all he could do for her.

He watched the man and the child walk falteringly across the clearing and he made no move toward them. As they came close he squatted so he was at eye level with the child. He didn't smile, but kept his eyes focused on her arm.

'Is it broken?' he asked, and the old man grunted assent from above.

'She said…it cracked.'

'I can help with the pain. If you'll allow.'

The old man spoke to the child in murmured dialect and the child listened. She hadn't taken her eyes from Grady.

'I need to give an injection,' Grady said softly, and the man interpreted to the child.

The little girl whimpered and backed away a little, but she didn't run.

'The injection will hurt a little,' Grady said. 'But then it won't hurt while I examine the arm. I can make sure the arm is straight and I can wrap it tightly so it won't hurt as much while it heals.'

More interpretation. He repeated himself a couple of times, a word at a time. And then he waited.

Silence.

He was very aware of the shadows. Scores of people watching from the shadows.

He waited, as if he had all the time in the world.

He waited.

Then there was a frightened whisper from the child to the old man and a one-syllable response, before the old man again addressed Reece.

'She wants that you are friend of Dr Morag. I told her yes.'

Grady nodded gravely. 'Thank you.'

'You can give her…injection,' the old man said. 'She knows a friend of Morag will not harm her.'

It went against everything Grady had ever been taught. To not X-ray…

He gave an injection of morphine and gently felt the fracture site. Then he held the child's arms out, measuring reach. He carefully tested each finger, each part of the arm, searching for nerve damage, searching for any sign that the bone had splintered.

It seemed OK. It was probably a greenstick fracture, but not to take an X-ray…

He had no choice.

He splinted the arm still and carefully strapped the arm to keep it immobile.

A cast would be better, but he couldn't apply plaster here. Besides, the arm was badly scratched and he was acutely aware of Morag's warning about infection. If there was infection under a cast and there weren't constant checks, she could well lose the arm.

Enough. He fashioned a sling and finally dared a smile at the little girl.

'You're very brave.'

The old man translated and the little girl's face broke into a grin. And what a grin! It was like the sun had suddenly come out.

'Than' you,' she whispered and Grady felt his gut give a solid wrench—a wrench he hadn't known he was capable of feeling.

'You're welcome.' He smiled at her, and then looked up to find his interpreter was also smiling. 'She must keep this on for six weeks. I'll come and check it.'

'Six weeks?' the old man repeated, and Grady nodded.

'She will keep it with care. But...Morag will check it. Not you.'

Right. Of course. This was Morag's place.

Not his.

After that he saw an ankle that he hoped—where was the X-ray?—was just sprained. Then there were two nasty cuts that needed careful cleaning and debridement. Amazingly, he was able to convince the children to accept tetanus shots and an initial shot of antibiotics. They'd need a ten-day course, but he left it to Morag to explain about the medication. Hell, if he explained it wrong...

He didn't stitch either of the cuts. He pulled them together with steri-strips as best he could, and told his interpreter that the strips could come off after a week. He hoped like hell that Morag would approve.

'How's it going?' She was suddenly behind him and he almost jumped. She was like a cat, moving among her own with a sureness that had him disconcerted.

'Fine,' he managed. 'Can you explain a course of antibiotics for these kids?'

'I can do that. One of the women's very good at dispensing medication. Nargal will explain it for me.'

'Nargal can't do it himself?'

'The tablets are food. That's women's work. Asking Nargal to make sure a child has a tablet twice a day would demean him.'

'I see.' He adjusted the dressing and smiled a farewell to the little boy, and looked uncertainly at Morag. He felt all of about six, asking, 'Please miss, have I done OK?'

'I had to use dressings,' he confessed.

'Sure you did,' she said, and then grinned. 'Heck, you look like I'm about to slap you.'

'You're not?'

'Argrel—the little boy with the first cut you treated—came to show his mother his bandage while I was with the women. He said the big doctor—I guess that's you—said he couldn't get it wet for three days. He explained to his mother that he wasn't allowed to get it dirty and in three days he could take the dressing off and he'd have a wonderful man scar.' Her smile widened. 'You certainly know the way to a small boy's heart.'

'Promising him scars.'

'Out here they're better than a jelly bean.'

They were smiling at each other—like fools. Which was really stupid.

'What next?' he asked.

'I'm finished.'

'Finished?' He frowned. 'Two lacerations, a broken arm and a sprained ankle?'

'I've strapped two fractures.'

'Nothing else?'

She hesitated. 'They did lose some of their people. There's nothing we can do there.'

'But there's no serious injuries.'

'Once again, not...not that we can do anything about.'

'What do you mean?'

'Two of the old people are badly injured,' she told him. 'One of the elderly men has a compressed skull fracture. He's deeply unconscious and his breathing's starting to weaken already. And there's an old woman with a fractured hip.'

He stared. 'So what are you going to do about it?'

'Nothing,' she said simply. She was collecting gear and tossing it into the back of the truck. Then she relented. 'No. I have been allowed to do something. I've left enough painkillers so Zai will drift toward death in peace.'

'For a broken hip?' he asked incredulously. 'We can take her back. Set it. And the compressed fracture—we could alleviate pressure—'

'You know as well as I do that if there's been pressure on the brain for twenty-four hours, the damage will be irreversible. And Zai…yeah, you're right, we could operate. But that means a trip to Sydney. She'd be in hospital for weeks, facing rehabilitation. She can't do that.'

'How fragile is she?'

'Not very.'

'Then why can't she do it?'

'She'd die,' Morag said simply. 'You put Zai in a Western hospital ward and she'd die of shock and terror.'

'So she'll die anyway?'

'Yes,' she said flatly. Dully. 'Of course she will. She knows that. But at least she'll die out here, surrounded by her people and the way of life that's been hers for ever. It's the way she wants it, Grady, and I'm not about to argue.'

'You can't just—'

But he wasn't allowed to continue. 'Yes, I can,' she snapped. 'Of course I can. These people have a way of life that I respect, and that way of life has nothing to do with the customs we hold dear. If this island's deemed uninhabitable…'

'They'll be resettled. Maybe they'd be better off on the mainland.'

'I don't think so.'

'Why not? At least they'd have medical facilities.'

'They have medical facilities now,' she said in a savage undertone that was laced with pain. It hadn't been easy, he guessed. To walk away from a patient she could have helped. 'They have me. I've worked so hard to get their trust, and I'm succeeding. OK, it's a tiny bit at a time, but I'm allowed to help the children. They call me now if a mother gets into major trouble during childbirth, and that's a huge concession. Even though I've no specific obstetric training, I can often help. And I'm certainly better than nothing.'

She gazed up at him, her eyes troubled, trying to make him see. 'They can't be isolated from our world for ever,' she admitted. 'But they can be assimilated ever so carefully, ever so gently, so they can preserve the values and traditions they value while taking the best of ours.'

'But to leave her to die... Morag, surely you don't believe—'

'Oh, for heaven's sake. Leave me be!' He was suddenly aware that there were tears welling up in her eyes and she swiped them away with an angry gasp. 'Do you think I like not being allowed to treat Zai? Don't you think I mind that an old lady I've known and respected since my father brought me out here twenty years ago is dying out there among the palms? And do you think I haven't thought these issues through again and again? Of course I have. But you...you're going to hold a public meeting in the next few days. I know you are. Marcus told me that's what the plan is. Give us a day or so to appreciate how deeply we're in trouble, and then you and the rest of the bureaucrats you work with are going to say close down that island, take these people to the mainland—they'll be better off. As if you know anything at all...'

She broke off. She gave an angry sniff and then another, but as he made a move to touch her she backed away as if his touch would burn.

'Don't touch me. We have to get back to town.'

'Morag—'

'Just...leave it. I've just said goodbye to two people I love. Leave me alone to get over it. You wouldn't know what that's like, Grady Reece. You fly to the rescue, you do your dramatic thing and then you leave everyone else to pick up the pieces.'

'Morag...'

She gulped. 'I'm...I'm sorry,' she managed. 'That's not fair. You've been...you've been an enormous help and I'm incredibly grateful. But can you imagine what sort of lives these people will lead if they're transplanted to the mainland? Can you?' She shook her head. 'No. I'm sorry. You can't have thought… And why would you? This isn't your business, Grady. Just leave me be to come to terms with it.'

CHAPTER EIGHT

THEY drove back to the village in unbroken silence. There were eggshells everywhere, Grady thought ruefully, and he wasn't sure where to tread. Where to go to from here?

Back to Sydney? Of course. In a couple of days. When the disaster was over.

Or when the disaster was just beginning...

He couldn't afford to think like that, he told himself. Could he?

In the meantime, silence seemed the only option.

They arrived back at the field hospital just as Lucy was being prepared for the helicopter flight to the mainland. Jaqui had been looking after her, and as Morag appeared in the hospital entrance, Jaqui looked up in relief.

'Lucy was hoping you'd be back before she left.'

'I've been out at the settlement,' Morag told the teenager.

'Are there more deaths out there?' Lucy whispered, and Morag took her hand and squeezed. Grady stood back with Jaqui, watching in still more silence. He was starting to feel impotent. There was nothing he could do. Nothing!

'There are,' Morag told her.

'My dad'll hate it.' Lucy hesitated. 'Nargal?'

'Nargal's fine.' She smiled, and turned to include Jaqui and Grady. 'Nargal shows Lucy's father the best place to fish. Lucy's dad found Nargal after his canoe was upended in a storm twenty years ago. Peter spent the night out searching when everyone else had given up. By the time he found him, Nargal had almost reached the end—he was far gone with hypothermia. But Peter brought him back and Nargal's been good to him ever since.' She hesitated and then turned back to Lucy. 'Nargal says his men are out looking for Hamish.'

106

'Everyone's looking for Hamish.' The girl's voice broke on a sob. 'I should be.'

'No. You shouldn't.' Morag ran her fingers down Lucy's face. 'You've lost skin all down your chest, your arm's broken and you're in no fit state to do anything but recuperate.' She motioned back to Grady and Jaqui. 'You know these two are part of the country's top Air-Sea Rescue team. If they can't find Hamish, no one can. We have hundreds of people combing the island and the sea.'

'He'll be drowned.'

'If he is,' Morag said gently, 'then it's even more important that you be with your parents. They'll be going out of their minds, Lucy. I know you can't do anything here, but you can be with them and, believe me, it's the most important thing. When you can't do anything else, you give yourself.'

Hell.

Grown men weren't supposed to cry.

Grady sniffed.

Jaqui cast him a suspicious glance and offered him an out. 'Dr Reece, Doug wants you in the control room,' she told him. And then, as he turned to leave, she pressed something into his hand. 'Don't forget your hanky.'

'So where the hell is he?'

'There's nothing else we can do, Grady.' Doug, their search and rescue chief, was looking grim as Grady emerged from his encounter with Lucy. 'We have to assume all the missing are drowned. The Kooris were all on the beach when the wave hit and we can assume Hamish was on the beach as well. There's been bodies washed in but if they were caught in currents, we need to accept the fact that we're never going to find them.'

'You're still searching?'

'It's been twenty-four hours. Surviving in the water for that long…'

'It's possible. Especially if they caught hold of debris.'

'Grady, it's been a really calm day. The water's like a pond.

Our visibility is great. We're checking every piece of debris in a twenty-mile radius—'

'Make it thirty.'

'Grady…'

'These are kids,' Grady said. 'Kids.'

'Grady, let's keep the emotion out of it,' Doug told him, giving him a curious glance. 'We're doing the best we can.'

'And long term?' he asked dully.

'Services are non-existent,' Doug told him. 'No power, no water, no sewerage. No money and no political clout. There's no long term for this island.'

That was blunt. Grady dug his hands in his pockets and stared out into the late afternoon light. From this point high on the cricket ground, he could see the devastation the wave had caused. There was so much destruction. To rebuild…

Morag would have to leave.

It was personal. He found his hands were clenched into fists deep in his pockets and Doug was staring at him as if he didn't recognise him.

'You OK?'

'Yeah.' He grunted an assent. 'Yeah, I am.'

'The powers that be want a health statement from you,' Doug told him. 'No water, no sewerage… You know the risks.'

'And the answers I give will mean this island goes under.'

'This island went under yesterday,' Doug said bluntly, and then looked skyward as a helicopter appeared on the horizon and started its descent. 'Here's the chopper for the girl. Maybe we could move some more people out on the same flight. The evacuation has to start some time.'

'Not yet,' Grady growled. A group of men were making there way up from the township and he recognised Marcus, the unofficial spokesmen for the townspeople. He was walking slowly, his shoulders slumped. Like a man defeated, Grady thought. Hell.

'Let's get everyone out who's medically unfit at least,' Doug urged, and Grady thought back to the old lady dying slowly and unnecessarily back at the Koori settlement.

'Let's not,' he muttered. 'Not yet.'

He paced.

The helicopter landed and took off again, half-empty. From where Grady stood he had watched as Jaqui and Morag had seen Lucy on board, handed her medical notes over to the flight team and then stood back while the chopper had roared off toward the mainland.

He watched as Jaqui turned and gave Morag a hug.

He wasn't the only one this situation was getting to, he figured. His team was trained to be dispassionate. Trained to get in hard, do what had to be done and get out again.

In two or three more days they'd have made a decision about evacuating the island. The place would be empty and he'd have moved on.

And Morag?

She'd have moved on, too. Back to Sydney?

He couldn't see it.

Did he want to see it?

It didn't matter, he thought heavily. It wasn't going to happen. He and Morag… No and no and no…

Jaqui was down there, hugging her. Damn, why wasn't he down there, hugging her?

Because he knew that if he touched her, he'd commit himself.

Hell, Reece! He gave himself a sharp mental kick. He didn't do commitment. At least, not to women who were caught up with small boys and islanders and who were going to blame him for every decision that was made about this island and…

This was really deep water.

He dug his hands still further into his pockets. Morag was walking back to the tents. There might not be a medical need back in the hospital beds, but there was certainly an emotional need. From the moment she'd appeared back from the settlement the rest of the med team had been telling Morag who desperately needed to talk to her. She was burdened as no woman should be, he thought savagely. How dared the islanders put such a load on her shoulders?

'She's quite a woman,' Jaqui said softly, and he jumped. He'd been watching Morag, and hadn't noticed his partner come up behind him.

'She's devastated,' he said, almost to himself. 'This island's finished.'

'It'd take a huge commitment to keep it going. One doctor's not going to cut it.'

'Not only one doctor. The infrastructure…'

'I know.' Like him, Jaqui was looking down at the ruined town. 'Did you know my husband's head of the Public Works Department in Sydney West? I've been talking to him about the vast effort it'd take to rebuild this place.'

'Huge.'

'It'd be such a project…' She cast him a look that was as curious as the one Doug had given him. 'How did you go with the Kooris?'

'They're…' He hesitated and then shrugged. Why not say it? 'They're fantastic. They take our medicine on their terms.'

'They wouldn't let me near,' Jaqui told him. 'But, oh, I wish…' Her voice trailed off and he knew exactly what she wished. He was wishing it himself.

'It's not going to happen,' he said roughly. 'They'll be relocated.'

'I'd imagine they'll refuse to be relocated,' Jaqui said. 'They'll stay here with no medical facilities at all, and all the good Morag's done will be undone.'

'It's none of our business.'

'No,' Jaqui said, with another curious sideways glance. 'Of course it's not. How can it be?'

There were still a couple of hours of daylight left. He could go back into the hospital and help Morag—but for most of the things she was doing she didn't need help. She'd be adjusting pain medication, talking through terrors, facing the future.

With her people…

The thought was unsettling and Grady wasn't sure how to handle it.

At least there was other work to be done. He took himself down the hill to where an army of people was sifting through sodden belongings, searching for some trace of a past that had been washed away.

Doug overtook him there and together they checked the smashed infrastructure as Doug talked him through the impossibility of rebuilding.

'OK, it's not possible,' Grady said at last. He gazed at an elderly woman in the ruins of what had obviously been the village church. The wave had gone straight through, leaving only a shell. Pews and fittings had been shattered into a pile of jumbled ruins. The nave, though, with its vast, east-facing window, was still almost intact. The window was without glass, but from where Grady stood he could see right to the ocean beyond.

The woman was staring outward, looking at the sea. Just…looking. In the midst of all this confusion, it was an incredibly peaceful scene, and Grady thought suddenly that there was little need for fittings. It was breathtakingly lovely, just as it was.

The woman turned and saw the two men, she gave them a faltering smile.

'The doctor. Just who I need. I have a splinter that's stopping me working.'

Grady crossed the ruins to meet her. She was none too steady on her feet, he noticed, and she let him take her arm and help her out to the remains of the church-ground. While Doug watched, he lifted her hand and saw a shard of wood had been driven right under the nail.

'I'll take you to the medical centre.'

'No.' She shook her head. 'I have too much to do to bother. But if you could pull it out…'

'It's in deep.'

'Just…pull.'

'I need to cut the nail.'

'Then cut it,' she said, and there was desperation in her voice. 'Now. Please. The pain's driving me crazy and I need to concentrate. Please, will you help me?'

He looked down at her, trying to figure how to argue, but what he saw in her face gave him pause. There was no argument. She wouldn't go to a medical centre. And the light here was good enough…

OK. He could do this. He always carried a fully equipped medical kit in his backpack, and in a way he welcomed something practical to do. At least this was something medical rather than medical administration.

The questions he and Doug were trying to find answers to were impossibly difficult. How long could villagers survive without a viable water source? What were the risks of disease if sewerage contaminated the groundwater?

Or maybe they weren't impossibly difficult. Maybe they were questions to which he knew the answers, but he didn't like facing them. The thought of Morag's reaction when she heard was dreadful.

Morag. He couldn't think of what she was facing. He didn't understand her fierce love for this little community but now at least he knew that her love was for real, and the dispersing of the islanders would break her heart.

Hell! He'd much rather face a splinter, complicated or not.

So, as Doug excused himself, he found himself perched on a low stone wall, carefully extricating a splinter from an elderly lady's finger.

Working with care, with her hand spread on the sun-warmed stones, he blocked her ring finger with local anaesthetic. Then he carefully sliced a wedge from her nail, lifting it free so he could reach the sliver underneath.

The woman—she said her name was May Rafferty but that was all she was saying—stared straight ahead as he worked and she didn't speak until he applied antiseptic and dressing and asked her about tetanus shots.

'They're up to date,' she said shortly. 'Morag sees to that.'

'I'd imagine she would.' He hesitated. The woman, in her late sixties or early seventies, lean and weathered, with the look of someone who'd seen a lifetime of hard work, was staring again through the ruins of the church toward the sea.

'I'm sorry about your church,' he told her.

'It'll be OK. We'll rebuild.'

Would they? Grady thought of the report he was preparing and he winced. But now wasn't the time to talk of that.

'My husband was buried from this church,' May said softly. 'And my baby daughter. That's how I got the splinter. There's a plaque somewhere that my husband carved when our baby died. I thought…I thought I might be able to find it.'

'Would you like me to help you look?' he heard himself say, and she nodded as if she'd expected no less.

'I'd be very grateful.'

So with all the work to be done—with the momentous decisions still hanging in the balance as to the fate of this island— Grady found himself hauling aside splintered timber and ruined furnishings, trying to reach the base of the west wall, trying to locate one tiny carving…

Like the technical medicine of removing the splinter, it was work that he welcomed. It let him stop thinking of Morag's face as she read the report.

Morag…

Enough. Stop thinking now!

He had thick leather gloves to work with, and the task was simple enough. From the sidelines the woman watched, still in silence. Without gloves, and with her injured hand, he wouldn't let her haul things aside, but her eyes still searched the ruins. Ceaselessly.

And when he hauled aside a section of what looked like a

door, she saw what she was looking for. She gave a soft moan of relief and darted forward to lift a plaque.

It was a battered piece of wood, a little less than a foot square, and it looked as if it had once been highly polished. The wave had battered it with force, marring the carving, but the lettering was still clear.

> *Morag Louise Rafferty*
> *29 July 1970–20 January 1971*
> *Precious infant daughter of May and Richard.*
> *Died of diphtheria, aged six months.*
> *A tiny life; a jewel;*
> *a love that will live for ever.*

May was cleaning the lettering with her sleeve, smiling down at it as if she'd found the child herself. And for the second time that day Grady found himself swallowing. Hard. Hell! He didn't do emotion. He didn't!

'Morag,' he managed after a while. 'Your little girl was called Morag?'

'Mmm.' She smiled mistily up at him. 'Your Morag was named after her.'

'My Morag?'

'The Morag you've been working with,' she explained. 'Your Morag's father was my second cousin. He was best man at our wedding, and he was our Morag's godfather. We're so intertwined, the two families. My son...' She clasped the plaque closer. 'My son Peter—my Morag's brother—married Christine. Christine's brother was David, the fisherman who married Beth, your Morag's sister. So Christine is Robbie's aunt.'

He thought it through. He was confused. Very confused. Genealogy wasn't his strong point, and the complexities of this island's relationships had his head spinning. But he finally thought he had it. 'So your son and his wife are Peter and Christine Rafferty, the couple we've evacuated to Sydney?'

'Yes.'

'Then Lucy—Lucy and Hamish…'

'Lucy and Hamish are my grandchildren.'

That had him even more confused. 'Then why…?'

'Why haven't I been with Lucy?' She shrugged and hugged the plaque against her, as if suddenly cold. 'Lucy didn't want me. She's so angry. So distressed. She said I should be out here searching for Hamish, and, of course, I have been. But there's nowhere else to search and your people are so much more competent, and suddenly…' She shivered again. 'I just wanted…'

She just wanted contact with her daughter, Grady thought with sudden insight. Her little one. This plaque was a tangible link with the past, a link to hold onto when the future looked dreadful. Grady could see it in her face and he let her be for a moment, waiting until she turned again to the east window. She gazed out to sea for a long moment, and finally her face regained a little of its serenity.

'You're all so intertwined,' he said softly. 'I'd thought…I'd thought when Beth died that Robbie had no one.'

'Robbie never had no one,' May said simply. 'Robbie has every single islander. There's no one here who wouldn't give the boy a home and be glad to do it. But Beth and Morag were sisters. They were very close. You don't mess with closeness like that.' It was said with such flat simplicity that there was no argument.

He tried to take it all in. He tried. 'This island's one big family.'

'It is,' May told him, and attempted a faltering smile. 'In a while…in a little while, when everyone who can be saved has been saved, then this church will be cleared and the funerals will start. When my Morag died, when Beth died, when Beth's husband David was drowned…every single islander was here to bid them farewell. It'll be no different this time. As long…' She faltered and then attempted to recover. She didn't quite make it. 'As long as they find Hamish,' she whispered. 'If he's drowned… They must find his body. They can bury him next to my Morag. I…'

But the thought of the loss of her grandson was suddenly overwhelming. She put a hand to her face and turned away. 'Enough. If there's any news, let me know. I'll be up at the tent place that everyone's calling home. Thank you for tending my hand.' She hugged the plaque again. 'And thank you for finding my…for finding my Morag. If I can't find Hamish…' She faltered again and closed her eyes, but when she opened them there was a calmness there. A strength. Generations of tragedy had touched this woman and would touch her further, but she was here, here with her people, and life would go on.

'Take care of your Morag,' she whispered. 'She needs it most.'

Doug was waiting in the background with more of his damned facts.

'It's impossible,' he said. 'There's no infrastructure. We'd have to pull in really top people from Sydney. This needs an engineer who really knows what he's doing to supervise, huge manpower to pull it off, tradesmen of all descriptions… Then there's the medical side. We have a situation where the entire island's been traumatised, including the local doctor. She's a single mum. She can't cope with this long term. The money…the commitment…'

'The islanders won't leave.'

'They won't have a choice,' Doug said bluntly. 'It's either abandon the island or be cut off from all services. You'll never get political support for the sort of funding this place needs. And you'll never get the personnel.'

He should go back to the medical centre. There was still an hour or so before dusk and Jaqui might need him. But Grady's radio was on his belt and he knew he could be contacted, so he found himself picking his way through the debris until he came to the promontory where the lighthouse stood.

Morag was there. As he'd hoped. He rounded the cliffs that separated the promontory from the township and he saw her, standing at the foot of the lighthouse, staring up at the white-washed tower.

David and Goliath.

That was what she looked like, he thought. A tiny figure, facing immeasurable odds.

He called and she turned, but she didn't smile. She simply watched as he made his way down the cobbled walkway that reached out to where the lighthouse tipped the promontory.

'I hoped I might find you here,' he said, but there still wasn't a smile.

'I need to put out some food for Oscar.'

Oscar. Of course. Sam's cat.

'He comes here?'

'He likes here,' Morag told him. 'Oscar's the most independent cat we know. He lives on Sam's boat but for some reason he thinks this is his territory, so he visits us each night.'

'Maybe he likes you,' Grady said gently, but he still didn't get a smile.

'Maybe.'

'You're exhausted.'

She nodded. 'And…defeated. So much death.'

'You need to go back to Robbie.'

'I just phoned him. He's OK. He understands. I just wish…I just wish he didn't have to.'

'Let me help you here and I'll walk you up to Hubert's'

'No.'

'No?'

'It doesn't help,' she whispered. 'If I learn to lean on you.'

There was nothing to say to that. He watched as she scooped a can of cat food out into a crevice beside the lighthouse walkway, out of sight of watchful seagulls but certainly in smelling distance of the tomcat if he cruised past later in the night.

She straightened and looked at him as if she couldn't quite

figure out why he was there. 'I need to check the light,' she told him, and it was a dismissal.

'I want to see.'

'Grady—'

'I know.' He held up his hands in mock surrender. 'I'm not helping. But I'm curious. I've never been in a lighthouse before.'

'It's not as good as it used to be.'

'Why not?'

She hesitated then shrugged, as if she didn't have the energy to tell him to get lost. Though her shrug said she'd certainly like to. 'The light used to be fantastic,' she told him. 'It was a huge Fresnel lens that once filled the lantern room.'

'Tell me about it.' More than anything, he ached to take that look of utter defeat from her face. He could think of no way to deflect her. But she must love this lighthouse.

And it seemed that she did.

'It was vast,' she told him. 'Wonderful. It had about a thousand individual glass prisms mounted in brass. It stood almost twenty feet tall and six feet wide, and was large enough for a man to stand inside. But now... Now we have a small green DCB-24 Aerobeacon. It's about a hundredth of the size, even though it can still be seen for almost eighteen miles.'

'Can we go up?'

'I guess...I guess we can,' she told him. 'At least, I can. I usually go up and check the light every couple of days. The globes change automatically—it's fully automated—but things still go wrong. Once I went up and a sea eagle had somehow smashed through the glass and was beating itself to death trying to get out again. I managed to get it out—amazingly it flew off and even looked like it might survive—but it had damaged the beacon.'

'You coped with a sea eagle alone?' he asked, stunned, and she looked at him as if he was stupid.

'Of course I did. What else was I to do?'

Scream and run? he thought. Call for Air-Sea Rescue?

That'd be him.

Call for him?

'I can go up now because the lamp's not burning,' she told him. 'After dusk you'll blind yourself.'

'I'd like to come.'

She gave him a dubious look. 'Aren't you supposed to be busy writing down all the reasons why the island should be declared uninhabitable?'

'Morag…'

'It's what you're doing, isn't it?'

And there was no answer but the truth. 'Yes.'

'Creep!'

'Don't shoot the messenger,' he said mildly, and got an angry glare for his pains.

'If people would support us—if the politicians realised how wonderful this place is…'

'You're too far from the mainland. Even the lighthouse doesn't need maintenance any more. It's been through a tidal wave without a blink.'

'Go jump, Grady.'

'Show me your lighthouse,' he told her. 'Please.'

'Fine,' she snapped. 'And then will you get out of my life?' She stomped forward and walked up the three huge stone steps to the lighthouse door, produced a key that was almost as big as her hand—and then paused. Instead of inserting the key in the lock, she simply pushed.

The lighthouse door swung wide.

'It's unlocked,' she said, and added, staring down at the lock, 'It's smashed.'

'The wave…'

'I checked yesterday. It was still locked and firm. This door's been built to survive battering rams.'

'It can't have been locked.' Grady wasn't really thinking of locks. He was thinking of Morag. Only of Morag. Of the way she looked…tired and defeated, yet still with shoulders squared and with the flash of fire in her words. Pure courage…

He'd thought it took courage to do what he did. Rescuing people from high seas, from burning buildings, from all sorts of peril.

But maybe Morag had needed a different kind of courage to do what she'd done over the past few years—and she'd certainly found it. In spades.

'It looks like someone's attacked the lock with an axe,' she was saying, and he hauled himself out of his preoccupation and moved forward to see.

She was right. The vast wooden door was intact, except for one slash, splintering deep into the lock.

Grady frowned and pushed the door further inward.

There was an axe propped against the wall where the spiral staircase started its long swirl upward.

'Who...?' Morag moved to the stair, but Grady stopped her.

'Let me go first.'

'The axe is down here,' Morag said reasonably. 'We're not about to get attacked.'

But Grady was already climbing, his face turned upward and his ears tuned to danger.

'If you're thinking it's a house burglar, there's not a lot of call for used aerobeacons,' Morag told him.

'Hush.'

'They're a bit strong for spotlighting rabbits.'

He smiled at that, but schooled his features to seriousness, turned and frowned her down. She was wonderful, he thought. Her humour shone through no matter how black things were. How could he have let her go four years ago?

But he needed to focus on other things beside Morag. 'Will you shut up, woman?'

'I only thought—'

'You didn't think enough. Hitting lighthouse doors with axes isn't a reasonable thing to do. So someone's acting unreasonably. Let's find out why before we treat this as a joke. We don't know if someone's here, but let's assume there is.'

And a hundred and twenty-nine steps later they had part of

their answer. The trapdoor up into the lantern room was securely bolted. From the other side.

Behind Grady, Morag had grown obediently silent. Her spurt of laughter had been as fleeting as any joy on this island this day.

Grady pushed the trapdoor upward but it didn't move. Frowning in concern, Morag edged him aside and knocked. Hard.

'Hello,' she called into the stillness. 'It's Morag. Dr Morag. Who's up there?'

The voice from above them responded immediately—a male voice, deep and gruff, with the hint of an educated English accent.

'Can you go away, please?' The man sounded distracted, almost panicked.

'William.' Morag seemed confused.

'Yeah, it's William,' the voice said. 'But, Morag, please…go away. I hadn't intended anyone to be here. I'm sorry, Morag. I'm sorry you have to…cope with this. Cope with me. But, please, let me be. I need to jump.'

CHAPTER NINE

THERE was a moment's deathly silence.

'Why?' Morag called sharply and urgently, as if William might jump at any minute. Which he might well do, Grady thought grimly. The pressure of onlookers could form an impetus to push a man hesitating on a death urge straight over the edge. 'William, tell us why.'

There was a moment's loaded silence. Dreadful silence.

'*Us?* Who's with you?'

Grady let his breath out. Contact established. The first hurdle crossed. He'd been involved in rescue efforts for intending suicides often in his career—taking people from ledges, rescuing them after they changed their minds, bringing them medical attention when a serious attempt didn't work—and he knew this first contact was vital.

Hauling people back from the abyss.

Often it didn't work. Too damned often. The hardest part of medicine was the life you couldn't save.

Morag had done the same training as he had, he thought grimly. She knew how important it was to establish empathy.

'Dr Reece is with me,' she called. 'Grady Reece. He's part of the rescue team.'

'William, I'm here to check out the lighthouse,' Grady said, interjecting just as strongly as Morag had. They needed to establish his presence was non-threatening. No one was going to burst in and haul him away from the edge. 'There's only the two of us. I persuaded Morag to bring me up to show me the light.'

'Grady, this is William Cray,' Morag told him loudly, as if she was performing an introduction. The last thing they wanted was for William to think they were whispering behind his back.

122

'*The* William Cray. William is the island literary celebrity. He wrote *Bleak Cradle* and…and…'

'And *Dog's Night* and *Evil Incarnate*.' Grady's mind was working fast as he made his voice sound excited. 'I know who William Cray is. Hey, I loved those books.'

'No one here reads them,' William said, softly now so they were struggling to hear.

'I read *Bleak Cradle*,' Morag told him.

'Did you like it?' William demanded, and Grady held his breath again.

'No,' Morag said honestly. 'You killed the heroine.'

Good answer. Honest answer. It was the sort of reply that engendered trust even further. William would know Morag wouldn't soft-soap him down.

But they could take this further.

'Hey, I liked it,' Grady told them, slightly indignant. 'I thought the heroine asked for what she got. What a dimwit. But the hero—what was his name? Demszel. Boy, you put him through some hoops.'

'You have read it.' William sounded disbelieving and Grady thought maybe he could play the affronted card.

'Hell, yes. Of course I have. Why would anyone not have? I've read everything you've written.'

'No one reads every one of mine.'

'I have.'

There was a moment's stunned disbelief. 'Tell me why Lucinda died.' A test.

He racked his brains. In truth, William's books were hardly his books of choice, but there were long, boring waits between rescues and a man couldn't play chess all the time.

'She made it with her sister's husband, and her kid was also her brother-in-law's kid, and the kid found out and…heck, it was really convoluted.'

Silence.

'Yeah, well, you'll be the only one who's read them.'

'Is that why you're planning on jumping?' Morag asked softly. 'Because you're depressed about your writing?'

'I'm not depressed about my writing.'

'Then what?'

'I'm not depressed.'

'You're not happy,' Morag said softly. 'Happy people don't think about suicide. Even in times like these. Can you tell us? William, will you explain?'

Keep him talking, Grady thought. Great going, Morag. If they could get him engaged…keep his mind off the jump…

'I'm just… Hell, it's all such an effort,' William was muttering. 'I've been fighting this for months now. Over and over. I can't think. I can't make myself do anything any more. Everything's just a huge effort. You know, just figuring out the commitment to ring my agent takes me days, and often I just can't do it. It's just…like living in black sludge. I can't move. And now my dog is dead.'

'You don't know your dog is dead,' Morag said sharply. 'They're still searching.'

'Yeah.' William's voice was a jeer. 'One dog. Twenty-four hours in the sea. You know, I would have killed myself months ago but for Mutt. He… Hell, he keeps me sane.'

'So if you jump now and Mutt's found, what are we going to do with him?' Morag asked.

'Get your nephew to keep him. And his friend. Hamish and Robbie, they're always pestering me to take him for walks.'

'You really think your Mutt would want to live with a nine-year-old rather than live with you?' Morag asked incredulously, and there was a moment's pause.

But then there was the sound of dragging—a door being opened above them—and Grady saw Morag wince. He guessed that William was opening the door to the ledge outside.

'William, you know we're both doctors,' he called, and there was another moment's silence, as though William was considering whether to answer them or not.

But finally he did.

'I know that. So you can help Morag with…with the mess. I need to—'

'You know you're suffering from depression.'

'I'm not suffering—'

'You are, mate,' Grady called urgently, knowing that time here was horribly limited. 'What you're describing sounds like real, dark and appalling depression. If I'm right, what you have is not just a bit of temporary sadness but a medically treatable, chemical imbalance. It's not just a bleak mood. It's depression as in a major clinical illness. Depression with a capital D—as in an illness that can be cured.'

'Cured…' There was a harsh laugh. 'Don't be funny. Cured. What a joke. It's been months. The times I've told myself to snap out of it…'

'It doesn't work, does it?'

'Of course it doesn't.'

'Treating yourself for this sort of depression is impossible,' Grady called. 'You can't do it. The more you try to tell yourself to snap out of it, the more you can't and the worse it gets. You feel a failure because you can't make yourself operate. You can't make the most minor decisions. You can't think forward with any glimmer of hope at all.'

'Yeah.' The door dragged again.

'But we can help,' Grady called strongly and urgently. 'It's not something you can cope with alone, but you can move forward. There's new antidepressants…'

'Yeah.' William's voice was a mocking cry. 'I've read about 'em. They knock you right out. You smile and wave but there's no one at home.'

'The old ones were like that,' Grady told him. 'Not any more. I swear. There's all sorts of people operating normal, optimistic lives while they're on antidepressants. While they're being cured. People you can't believe would ever need them. Depression's insidious and everywhere. They call it the black dog. William, believe me, it's treatable, and we can help you.'

Silence.

'It'd be an awful shame,' Morag said softly into the stillness, 'if we found Mutt tonight and you weren't here to welcome him home.'

Another silence. And then a rasping sob, choked back.

'If I go away,' Grady said, casting an urgent look at Morag. 'William, if I go downstairs, will you open the hatch to Morag?' He hesitated. 'It's over to you, mate. We're here to help. I swear we can help.'

'You can't.'

'Will you give us the chance? For Mutt's sake at least?'

'I...'

'Look, I'm going down,' Grady called, with a silent, urgent message to Morag. They had to act fast while William was hovering in indecision. Endless talk wouldn't help—not when there was no eye contact. The longer he stayed up there... Well, it was over to Morag. 'I'll stay down below,' he called. 'Either to scrape what's left of you off the rocks or to welcome you down when you come down with Morag. Your call. Over to you, Morag. See you below, mate.'

He turned and deliberately started the long climb down the stairs, allowing his boots to scrap on the worn steps so William could hear him going.

Please...

And before he'd gone twenty steps he heard the trapdoor being dragged back.

Morag was being allowed to enter.

He was brilliant.

With Grady present, William might have maintained a front. He might have played the man. But with Grady gone, all pretence disappeared and as Morag climbed the last few steps into the lightwell, he crumpled against her.

William had been one of the two men Morag had dated in the years she'd been back on the island. For a while things had looked possible, but in the end... He was trying really hard not to be gay, William had told her, and she'd decided pretty fast that this wasn't a strong basis for a relationship.

Plus, there was the fact that he hadn't made her heart flip as Grady had.

No one had. Ever.

But now… Morag knew William enough to hug him and to smooth his hair and hold him close until the ragged sobs subsided. This had been a serious attempt at suicide. She was under no illusion that if she and Grady had arrived ten minutes later they would have found a body at the base of the lighthouse.

But now…thanks to Grady…

She couldn't think about Grady. She needed to focus on William.

How much of his isolation had been caused by undiagnosed depression? she wondered. He held himself aloof and most of the islanders thought he was an intellectual snob. Once she had him started on antidepressants, would it be possible to pull him more into island life? Have him help in the planning for the rebuilding? Run a course for islanders interested in creative writing? Maybe…

Maybe nothing. There wasn't going to be an island, she told herself.

It was finished.

But now wasn't the time to say that. She held him for as long as he needed her. Finally William hauled back and looked at her with a smile that was half-ashamed. 'I've been a fool.'

'You've been ill,' she told him. 'You are ill. I should have seen it. I should—'

'You'd blame yourself?'

'Heck, William…'

'I'm a grown man. It's up to me to ask for help.'

'Are you asking for help now?' she asked, and there was a long silence. She met his look square on and waited—for however long it took.

And finally it came.

'Yes,' he said. 'Yes, I am.'

Marcus was waiting with Grady when they emerged from the lighthouse. They walked out the door and William put up a hand as if to shield his eyes from daylight. He'd walked up these stairs expecting never to climb down, Morag thought, and it must be quite a challenge to start again.

And here were Grady and Marcus. Marcus had been a tower of strength over the last twenty-four hours. The big fisherman seemed to be everywhere, organising, helping, planning. As Morag led William out the door, the two men she'd leaned on most were sitting on the stone coping, soaking the last rays of the day's sun.

What had Grady told Marcus about William? she wondered. Whatever it was, there was no judgement on Marcus's face. He peeled his long body off the stones and gave William a smile.

'I've been looking for you.'

'Is it Mutt?' William asked hoarsely, and Marcus's smile faded. There were islanders frantic about their loved ones, but for many, especially those who lived alone, the fate of their pets was just as important.

'No, mate,' he said gently. 'We haven't found your dog. But we're still looking. The reason I've been searching for you is that we're trying to sort out a bit of privacy for those who are in urgent need of it. Your cottage is one of the few that are undamaged. You have a water tank, a septic tank for sewerage and you have two bedrooms. We're wondering if you could take in old Hazel Cartwright. You know Elias was killed and her home is shattered. She's in the dormitory tent, just…just sitting. Your place is just up the hill from hers and she could still see the harbour. She can go to her daughter in Sydney if you refuse, but she's desperate to stay for as long as she can.'

Had Grady done this? Morag flashed him an uncertain look. One look at his impassive face made her sure that he had. Of all the… This was perfect. To give William a need…

For the next few days, until antidepressants could take effect, William needed constant supervision. In a city, Morag would recommend that he become a voluntary patient in a clinic specifically designed for those at risk of self-harm. Here there could be no such supervision.

But caring for Hazel... It might work. She could even talk to Hazel about William's needs, and they could care for each other.

Would he do it?

He was having trouble taking it in, she thought. She let her hand lie in his, aware that he was in need of support himself. To ask him to support another...

Would his black depression make him too self-absorbed?

'Hazel plays the piano,' William said softly. 'I've heard her. Mutt and I walk past her place on the way to the beach, and there's always music.'

'They said she could have been a concert pianist if she'd stayed in the city,' Morag told him. 'But she chose a life with Elias, a life on the island.'

'I have a piano,' William said, and Morag cast a fleeting glance at Marcus and guessed he'd already thought this out.

'Would you do it, mate?' Marcus said, ignoring the fact that Morag was still holding William's hand.

William stared at Marcus. Then he turned and stared up at the lighthouse. Finally he released Morag's hand and gave himself a shake, as if he was shaking off a cloak. A cloak of fog and darkness and despair...

'Of course I will,' he said. 'I'll come with you now, shall I, and ask her if she'll be my guest.'

Grady promised to call at William's in an hour with medication and for a talk. To check on Hazel, he said, but they both knew it was more than that. Marcus and William started back to the makeshift township, and Morag and Grady were free to talk.

But for a while there was silence. Morag stared after them

as if she couldn't believe her eyes. Finally she turned and asked the question that was slamming through her mind.

'Was that you?'

'Sorry?'

'Was that chance—or did you play a hand?'

'I might have,' he acknowledged, with the hint of a rueful smile.

'How?'

'Marcus came here at a run,' he told her. 'Apparently William left a note saying what he wanted done with his possessions. It was pinned to his front door. The nextdoor neighbour was curious and took a look. She panicked and gave the note to Marcus.'

'So Marcus knew William intended suicide. He never let on.'

'Do you think he should have?'

'No.'

'We're agreed the note blew off in the wind and no one ever saw it,' Grady told her. 'Marcus will square it with the neighbour.'

'And Hazel?'

'Once Marcus calmed down about William—there wasn't much either of us could do with the pair of you locked in the tower—he sat down and talked to me about the worst of his concerns. Hazel was top of the list.'

Morag sighed. So many things…so many worries… 'Hazel's a wonderful old lady,' she told him. 'She's played the church organ for ever. Whenever anyone's in trouble there's always been Hazel. We all love her.'

'Including William?'

'He might. Our William might just learn to love. He might just figure out there's different forms of loving and they don't all have to do with sex. I'll start him on antidepressants tonight. I guessed a while back that he was depressed but until now he hasn't let me close.'

Enough. She sat down beside Grady on the stones and turned

her face to the setting sun. Her shoulders slumped. She'd been so afraid...

'This island's all about loving,' Grady said softly, and she closed her eyes.

'It is.'

'I've been talking to May.'

'She's another wonderful lady.'

'This island breeds their women wonderful,' he murmured, and she grimaced. Then she opened her eyes again. She took a deep breath and faced what was coming.

'Yeah, right.' She stared down at her feet, as if her rough walking shoes could provide an answer. 'What will happen to the islanders?'

'I'm sure the spirit of the place will go on,' he said uneasily.

'What—in five hundred different locations, wherever we're dispersed?'

'The tentative plan is to relocate the bulk of the population to Port Shelba,' he told her. 'There's a big migrant centre there that's not being used. We can take that over as temporary accommodation until permanent housing's organised. The harbour there is under-utilised. The government would be prepared to give land grants, building grants, fishing licences—basically anything it takes to get families resettled.'

'You must really want this island evacuated.'

'They,' he said heavily. 'Not me.'

'You work for them.'

'I'm just an emergency services doctor, Morag.'

'You're a spokesperson for the government.'

'OK,' he said, gazing out into the fading light at the greyness of the sea and not at her. 'You tell me what's wrong with the plan. It sounds good to me.'

'It's terrible.'

'Why?'

'We're islanders,' she told him. 'We have our own heritage. Port Shelba's big. We'd be integrated into the broader population and our sense of community would be lost.'

'Is that important?'

'You've seen the damage depression can do,' she told him. 'Look what just happened here. Depression… You know, I've been working on this island for four years now and William's will be the first antidepressant I've prescribed. And that's only because he's a relative newcomer and he's held himself so aloof.'

'You've been lucky.'

He didn't have a clue, she thought bleakly. Not a clue. 'No,' she snapped. 'I haven't been lucky. I've been part of a community, but you don't know what that means, do you, Grady Reece? You can't possibly see how important that is. Without the community Hubert would be dead by now. The community keeps him alive and interested and involved. And what about the Kooris? How is the government planning on resettling them?'

'They're not.' This was the hard part and Grady stared out to sea some more. 'The Kooris won't move. We know that. But…maybe they don't want what's being offered even now in the way of health services. They're fiercely independent.'

'Oh, right.' Her anger was building to the point where she felt like kicking someone. Kicking Grady? Maybe. 'So because they're independent, you'd abandon them completely.'

'Of course not. We'd make provisions.' He met her look, her anger meeting his calm, placid response. As if he was really making sense. 'Morag, if you came to Sydney with me…'

Her breath stopped right there. 'What?'

'I love you, Morag,' he told her, so softly that she had to strain to hear what he was saying. And then he said it again, louder. 'I love you. I've fought against it all this time. Hell, if I knew how much it'd hurt four years back, I'd never have let you walk away.'

There was a deathly silence. 'You didn't have a choice,' she whispered at last, her anger sucked right out of her. 'You didn't let me go. I came all by myself.'

'But you didn't want to come,' he told her. 'Not really. Oh, you had no choice, I accept that. You loved Beth and you love Robbie and you care for this damned community.' He reached out and gripped her hands, urgently, as if he could somehow impart his message through touch.

'But, Morag, it's finished,' he told her. 'You've done a fine job. A wonderful job. These people…what you've built… I'm so proud of you.'

'Gee, thanks.'

He wasn't listening. 'Morag, we could build a life back in Sydney. I know you want to keep up with your medicine. And I'd be blind not to see your commitment to the Koori people. So what I suggest is—'

'What do you suggest?'

He caught her anger then, and frowned. 'Don't you want hear?'

'Of course I want to hear.'

'You'd bring Robbie with you,' he told her. 'That's understood. He's a great kid. He loves you and I'm sure…' He hesitated a little, but only just. 'I'm sure that I could be…more than a friend to him. I'm willing to try, Morag. For you.'

Her anger wasn't dissipating a bit. 'That's big of you.'

'Just listen. Morag… The Kooris…' He was trying so hard to make her see. She was listening to him and hearing his urgency, knowing that he was trying to make a case but not recognising that her heart was closed. It had to be closed. 'You could be the remote medical officer for them,' he told her. 'There'd be ample funding. With what the government saves in providing the infrastructure for this settlement, they'd be more than happy to spend in employing you. You could fly out here once every couple of weeks and do clinics at need. They'd still be in contact.'

'Every two weeks?'

'We think that's workable.'

'And if a woman goes into labour? You'd say she should wait two weeks for attention?'

'She'd have to come to Sydney before she was due.'

'She wouldn't.' She hauled her hands back and stared at him as if he was someone she'd never seen before. Someone she could never, ever understand.

Someone she could never love?

'Then maybe…' He hesitated. 'Morag, the Kooris chose this lifestyle. Maybe the risks come with the territory.'

Love didn't come into this, she thought bleakly. How could she think about loving this man when he was speaking such nonsense?

'They didn't choose this lifestyle,' she snapped. 'And now we've introduced them to a different one. We—my father and then Beth and now me—have taught them to trust. They bring the worst of their illnesses in their young to me now. The major traumas. And in childbirth, if there's a need, they come to me now. You'd take that away?'

'There's no choice, Morag,' he said flatly. 'Do you think you could get political support to rebuild this place?'

'Not without help.' She knew that. But that was all she knew.

And what help? She didn't even know who she needed.

The bleakness in her heart was growing by the minute.

'You don't have help,' he told her. 'Morag, you're so alone. It's crazy.'

'I'm not alone. I have all these people. Marcus. May. Hazel. Five hundred people who are part of me.'

'Those people are leaving.'

'But not the Kooris.'

'That's their choice.'

'And you think I have a choice?' she whispered. 'You want me to leave?'

'Yes,' he said, sure of his ground in this most important question. 'Yes, I do.'

'Why?'

'Because it's impossible here. And more…' He was standing before her now, and he was suddenly closer, his body language urgent. She'd also risen, glaring at him against a backdrop of setting sun. He reached out to take her by the waist but she stepped back.

'Morag, we've lost so much time,' he said. 'You've given this community four years and they can't expect any more. It's time to move on. Time to come back to me. Morag, I love you.'

It needed only this. Grady loved her? Still? And he was offering her a life.

So... She could walk away from her islanders, she thought dully. She could leave right now. She and Robbie could leave this island, go back to the life she thought she'd chosen all those years before.

How could she tell Robbie that they were leaving?

She might not have a choice. If the island truly was evacuated... If his best friend was dead...

But these were *her* people. If the island was evacuated, how damaged would they be? How much more would they need the doctor they'd leaned on for years? It wasn't just her. She was part of a dynasty of trust. Her father and then Beth and now her.

Take away their homes? Take her away as well?

No. She couldn't leave them.

'Grady, this isn't going to work,' she said softly. 'Not now.' She glanced around at the mess the wave had made of the shoreline and she shuddered. 'Look, we're talking about the future here—and the present's such a catastrophe that we can't even think straight. Can we just get on with it?'

'But you and I—'

'There's no you and me.'

'There is.'

'Grady...'

'Morag, I was mad to ever let you go,' he said strongly. 'I can't imagine why I did.'

'I didn't give you a choice.'

'You're saying you didn't regret it?'

'No. I...'

'You're saying you don't love me?'

She stared at him. He was so…capable, she thought desperately. Strong, competent and a little bit…dangerous? Ruthless?

He had all the answers, she thought, anger surfacing as it had four years ago. He'd take over her life and he'd put it back on track. Organise. Order.

Her life would be great. Robbie's life would be great. He'd care for them and make them laugh and make love to her and make her toes curl and the world would be a funny, happy, busy…

Her community would be without her. May. Hazel. Marcus and Judy and the kids. Angie Salmon, who'd hardly started to grieve.

'No.'

'Morag…'

'Grady, please. Don't ask.'

'I must.' His hands came out and caught hers. 'Morag, what's between us…it's irreplaceable. Four years ago I thought it was…not all that important. I thought I'd meet someone else. But there's only you. Morag, I can't bear to let you go again. We'll get the island evacuated—'

'No!' She was almost yelling at him now. Fear was surfacing behind the anger. Fear that she was losing control. She was losing her direction and it was desperately important that she find it again.

'Why not?' he said, his voice gentling.

'I can't. How can you not see?'

'I see what's between us.'

'There's nothing between us.'

'Don't be so…'

'So what?' She was close to tears. She was close to breaking and it must be obvious. Grady's face changed and suddenly instead of urgency there was tenderness. Compassion.

Love.

'Morag…'

There it was again. The way he said her name. It had the capacity to shift her off her bearings. It had the capacity to…

To weaken?

For suddenly she felt herself being drawn into him. Against her better judgement—against any sort of judgement—she was allowing those big, capable hands to pull her against him. Her breasts were pressing against the strength of him. His hand was cupping her chin and tilting her face.

And then…

He smiled down at her, a rueful, searching smile that asked more questions than it answered. And she couldn't reply. How could she reply as his mouth lowered onto hers?

She could drown in this kiss.

Four long years…

She'd thought she was over it. No. No, she'd never thought she was over it, she thought desperately, but she'd pushed away the feel of him. The scent of him. The pure animal magnetism…

Her love for this man was so real. It was an aching need that had had her crying out in her sleep for the first twelve months of her stay on the island. Her dreams of her dead sister had been crazily mixed with her need for this man,

Loss. She'd lost so much. Her loss was real and dreadful, and the sudden lessening of it, the sudden glimmer of hope that her loss wasn't irrevocable, had her responding now as if her body had known all along that this was her rightful place.

This was her home. This man was her man, and the only place in the world that she could ever be at peace was right here.

Within the arms of the man she truly loved.

So for one long moment she melted into his kiss. For one glorious moment she let herself surrender to the promise of his body. To the feel of his hands, pulling her into him. To the feeling that here in his arms anything was possible. With Grady beside her, she could take on the world. Save her island. Find Hamish safe and well. Care for the Kooris.

With Grady she could do anything. She could fly!

Above her head the light from the lighthouse shimmered on, automatically powered to light up with the gathering dusk. The flash of light across her face was hardly enough to haul her back from insanity—it didn't—but it was enough to make her catch a trace of reason. To haul back. To gasp and push back with both hands. To stand and stare with eyes that were wild with want and hope and aching, tearing need.

And above all…despair?

'Grady, don't…'

'You want—' he started in a voice that was far from steady.

'What I want doesn't come into it,' she whispered. 'This is crazy. A tidal wave washes away the foundations of my community and you're saying I should leave them? I can't. Grady, don't ask me.'

'Morag—'

'Leave it,' she said, roughly and despairingly. 'Go back from where you came, Grady. You're needed in a crisis. Medical emergencies. But what I do… I don't do emergencies, Grady. I do for ever.'

She stared at him for one long moment, as though taking in everything she could about him. One long, last look…

'I need to go home,' she whispered. 'I'm sorry, Grady. I have to go back to Robbie.'

And before he could say another word she'd turned and fled, back to where the track started its winding way up toward Hubert's cottage.

Back to the community where she belonged.

CHAPTER TEN

GRADY walked back to the hospital and met Jaqui about to organise a search party. He'd turned his radio off during the conversation with William and hadn't turned it on again—a transgression that had every member of their team concerned. Briefly he outlined what had happened, but halfway through she interrupted.

'You mean he jumped?'

'No.'

Her eyes narrowed. 'But you look like something dreadful's happened.'

'It hasn't.' He gave a rueful smile. 'Morag wouldn't let him jump. She's better than any psychiatrist.'

'She's a damned fine doctor,' Jaqui told him. 'The islanders think the world of her.' She hesitated, and eyed him sideways. He knew she could see there was still something badly askew in his world—but she didn't press further.

'The reason we were trying to find you was that the politicians want to fly in tomorrow for a public announcement.'

'That the island's to be evacuated?'

'You helped Doug make his report.'

'I did,' he said heavily.

'There's health risks in not doing it fast,' Jaqui told him. 'You know it. The water source is contaminated. If we're not careful we could have a great little epidemic of typhoid. Just what we all need—I don't think.'

'If we could get the resources—'

'They aren't available.' She hesitated, and gave him that questioning look again. And obviously decided to push it. 'And, besides, this way you'll get your girl.'

'What the hell is that supposed to mean?'

'I mean you're nuts on your Dr Morag,' she told him bluntly. 'Any fool can see that. If the island's evacuated, it means she'll have to leave, too.'

'She won't *have* to do anything.'

'Is that what you were doing?' Jaqui asked slowly. 'Is that why you look like you do? Because you were asking?'

'Jaqui…'

'Just enquiring,' she said thoughtfully, throwing her hands up in defence. 'OK, moving right on…' She gave him a grin that contained real affection. 'Do you have time to assist in removing an appendix?'

'An appendix?' He stared.

'You wouldn't read about it.' Her grin widened. 'After all we've gone through. Mary Garidon is fifteen years old, and she's been clutching her stomach since the wave hit. Her parents assumed it was stress and maybe I'd have agreed with them if I'd seen her earlier. But her mum came in to get the haematoma on her thigh checked. She was caught by the end of the wave. Anyway, Mary was waiting with her father, and her dad was telling her to pull herself together. But she looked sweaty and was clutching her stomach so I checked. She's got rebound, Grady.'

'Rebound…' He stared. 'You mean the appendix has ruptured?'

'That's what it looks like. I think we should go in now. Can you help?'

'Of course.' If the appendix really had burst, the time taken to evacuate her to Sydney could well mean the infection would be much worse.

'I was hoping you'd be back,' she confessed. 'You've got the best fingers I know.'

'Gee, thanks.'

'You don't want to call Morag? She's Morag's patient.'

'The whole island is Morag's patient,' Grady growled. 'Everyone needs her.'

'Including you?'

'Butt out, Ford.'

She grinned. 'When have I ever? But we don't contact Morag?'

'She's had a hell of a day. She's just talked someone out of jumping, and her kid must be going nuts without her. Let her be.'

'There's a real load on her shoulders,' Jaqui said seriously. 'Do you think she'll be happier without it?'

'When it's hauled out from under her?' Grady grimaced. 'No.'

'Even with you?'

'I said butt out. Her future's none of our concern.'

But as they scrubbed and prepared the teenager for surgery—as Grady reassured the frightened parents and promised them Morag would come if there was the slightest hint of trouble—as he performed the procedure with his trained anaesthetist and his two trained nursing staff and thought how Morag would have had to do this alone—somehow—if he and his team hadn't been here—he thought, How could her future be none of his concern?

He was going to worry about her for ever.

Morag made her way slowly up the scree. She flicked her radio transmitter back on to check in with Jaqui, who briefly outlined what was happening to Mary.

'Do you want me to come?' Morag had paused at a bend in the track and was involuntarily turning.

'We're fine. Two doctors, two nurses, one appendix. We have it under control.' There was a moment's hesitation and then Jaqui asked, 'How do you cope with something like this when you're on your own?'

'I talk one of the nurses through the anaesthetic,' she told her. 'I have no choice.'

'It's real bush medicine.'

'It's better than no medicine at all.'

'Do you enjoy it?' Jaqui asked curiously.

Morag hesitated. 'Yes,' she said at last. 'Yes, I do. To go back to ordinary medicine…'

'Like our Dr Reece stopping swinging on rescue harnesses.' Jaqui chuckled. 'A life lived on the edge. You two suit so well.'

'We don't,' Morag said quietly, and clicked off the receiver before she could hear Jaqui's next comment.

We don't.

Robbie would be desperate for her.

The little boy had been so good. To ask a nine-year-old to stay calmly up at Hubert's cottage while there was so much going on below—and when there was still no word of Hamish—must have been unbearable. She'd radioed him constantly during the day and each time his voice had sounded more and more strained.

'When will you come? Where's Hamish? Can't I come down?'

He and Hubert had done a wonderful job. The media circus was confined to the hills and she'd heard indirectly that Robbie had given the same interview over and over.

'The old man gives a nice artistic embellishment or two,' one of the reporters for the national broadcaster had told her when she'd finally agreed to a fast telephone link. 'But the kid…he's amazing. He'll be on the national news tonight.'

And he wouldn't be able to watch it, Morag thought ruefully. If she'd had time, maybe she could have phoned her mother on the mainland and had Barbara tape it for her.

Her mother… She hadn't heard from her mother, she thought bleakly. Would Barbara even know there'd been a tidal wave on Petrel Island?

Would Barbara care?

She trudged on upward. Once upon a time she'd thought she could lead the sort of life her mother led, where career and appearance were everything. She'd changed so much. She'd changed and Grady had stayed the same.

But she loved him…

She couldn't think of Grady. The moon wasn't yet over the horizon and it was deeply dark. She needed to concentrate on her footing.

The candle wasn't in Hubert's window.

Frowning, she quickened her steps, and suddenly a wavering flashlight appeared from the cottage door. The beam circled wildly and found her. It was a cameraman, his bulky equipment draped round his neck. There were a score of reporters and cameramen camped out near the helicopter landing pad. What was this man doing here?

Why wasn't the candle lit?

'Who are you?' she demanded, more sharply than she'd intended, and he blinked as if he was trying to adjust to reality.

'Dave Barnes. National Reporting.'

'What are you doing here?'

He peered at her, trying to see in the light from the flash, and she hauled her backpack from her shoulders and found her own torch.

'I'm Dr Lacy,' she told him. 'Morag Lacy. Where's my nephew?'

'You're a doctor?'

'Yes.'

'Thank God for that.' He grabbed her arm and practically hauled her into the cottage. 'We're camped behind the ridge but the old man said earlier that we could take a shower here if we wanted. I came down and the old guy and the kid were arguing. I went for a walk along the ridge to catch the last of the sunset, and when I came back he was like this.'

Like what? Who? But Morag was inside the cottage and through to the bedroom, and what she saw made her stop in dismay. 'Hubert!'

'I found him on the floor and for a minute I didn't think he was breathing,' Dave told her. 'I was just thinking I'd have to do CPR and then he groaned. Hell, I was glad to hear it. I've got him on the bed but he looks awful.'

He did. Hubert's gaunt face was staring up in terror as he

clutched his left arm. He was sweating profusely. Morag placed her fingers on the pulse in his neck, and his skin was cold to the touch.

At least she had equipment. Morag's doctor's bag was huge. Vast. It was twice the size of most doctor's bags but it hardly ever left her back and she had never been more glad of it than she was now.

'It's…it's a heart attack?' Hubert whispered. Behind them the cameraman was doing his best to hold the flashlight steady, but his hands were shaking. The beam was erratic, a wavering and eerie light across the bed of the sick man.

'Maybe it is.' She undid Hubert's shirt and placed her stethoscope on the old man's chest. His heartbeat was reasonably stable, she decided thankfully, though every four or five beats were slightly irregular—maybe ectopic? She hauled more equipment out of her bag, searching for aspirin. 'Put the flashlight on the dresser,' she told the cameraman. 'See if you can aim it so it's pointing at this arm. I need a glass of water. And there are candles somewhere in the kitchen.'

'First cupboard on the left,' Hubert quavered. 'And matches. I was just about to light them when…when…'

'Hush,' she told him. But this was good. If he had the strength to think about candles…

'Hell, it hurts,' he whispered, and reached out and clutched her arm. 'It hurts to breathe. Morag, I don't…I don't want to die. Not yet.'

'How about that?'

She even smiled as she adjusted the blood-pressure cuff and then had to force herself to stay smiling as the results told her that dying was a possibility. Eighty on fifty. There was definitely something nasty going on.

The cameraman returned with a large glass of water. She tipped three quarters of it out the open window and broke her soluble aspirin into what was left, swirled the water until the aspirin had dissolved and then held Hubert so he could swallow.

'Let's get it into you,' she told him. 'If you really don't want to shuffle off this mortal coil, drink this.'

'What is it?' He peered into the glass in deep suspicion.

'Really high-tech medicine. Otherwise known as aspirin. It acts as an anticoagulant, letting the blood flow a bit more easily. Maybe there's a slight blockage…'

'Slight? How can this be slight?' He sounded affronted and she smiled again.

'If it wasn't slight, you'd be dead.'

'Gee, thanks.' He grimaced but his lips managed to twitch. 'That's a real comfort.'

'I'll give you something for the pain.' Five milligrams, she decided, and then looked at the sheen of sweat on his forehead and thought, No, he was cracking hardy. Seven.

Behind her, the cameraman was setting up candles, working quietly and efficiently. His hands appeared to have steadied and Morag blessed him for it. You never knew with onlookers. Sometimes you got calm, intelligent help, as this man was providing, and sometimes you got panic. She'd learned early not to expect anything of anyone. A flighty teenager might be far more help than her sensible middle-aged father.

'Will I live?' Hubert faltered, and she rested her fingers on his pulse again.

'You've lived through a darned sight more than a mild heart attack,' she told him. 'But I need a cardiograph to tell any more than we already know. Hubert, we're going to have to take you to the pavilion.'

'To that makeshift hospital you've set up?'

'Yes. We have everything there we need.'

She even had Grady.

'I can't be sick. There's the public meeting tomorrow about the fate of the island,' he said fretfully. 'I gotta be there for that.'

'Let's just concentrate on tonight,' she said softly. 'For the moment, more than anything else you need to relax. Please. There are others who will worry about the island for you.'

'You'll fight for it?'

'Of course I will.'

'But Robbie...' His eyes widened, as if remembering something the pain and the shock had driven from his mind. 'I forgot Robbie. Hell, Morag, I shoulda been taking care of him. I need to...' He struggled to rise but she pressed him back.

'No. You're not to fret about Robbie. I'll take over his care now.' She bit her lip. Where was he? 'I've left him alone too long,' she said softly. 'He's been so good. But, Hubert, you've been wonderful, too. Now it's time to hand over the care to others.'

She passed her radio to the cameraman behind her. 'This is set to contact the medical team at the pavilion,' she told him. 'The hospital's commandeered about the only two workable vehicles on the island and I need one. Tell them we need transport to take Hubert down to the hospital. Tell them it's a suspected coronary.'

'Can do.' The man backed into the kitchen, obviously grateful for the chance to escape from the sickroom.

'I need to tell you about Robbie,' Hubert whispered, but there was a weariness in his voice that told Morag he was past worrying about anything but the beating of his own heart.

'Don't worry.' Robbie had been here a few minutes ago, Morag thought. The cameraman had seen him arguing with Hubert. If he'd seen Hubert collapse, he'd be dreadfully upset. Maybe he'd run to try and find her.

Damn, she couldn't do anything about Robbie. Not now. Not yet. The medical imperative...

She had to get Hubert stabilised. Hubert's life was under threat and the fact that her small nephew was distraught couldn't be allowed to interfere. But it hurt.

Grady. She needed Grady—now!

But she also needed to concentrate. Somehow Morag worked on, adjusting drips, monitoring, waiting. Often pain like this was a precursor to a main event. The aspirin would help—maybe.

Please…

Not another death, she found herself begging. Not Hubert. OK, he was ninety-two, but she wasn't ready to say goodbye to him yet.

And if Robbie thought he was somehow responsible… For him to carry that on his shoulders…

No!

Finally, with the drip steady and the old man drifting toward sleep as the morphine took hold, she was able to focus on something other than imperative need. She stepped back into the kitchen and found the cameraman putting down her radio.

'Dr Reece is busy,' he told her. 'Apparently there's been an emergency appendicectomy. But they're sending a truck.'

Her heart sank. Of course. The appendix.

No Grady.

Well, what was so unusual about that? she asked herself harshly. She'd been used to it for four years. She needed to get used to it again.

Robbie…

'The child who was here,' she ventured. 'Do you know where he is?'

The man smiled. 'He's a great kid, isn't he? He gave us some fantastic footage.'

'But…'

He got her worry then, and his smile died. 'I'm sorry. They were arguing as I arrived.'

That was what she didn't understand. Robbie didn't argue. At least, not with Hubert.

'I overheard it as I walked up the scree,' the man said apologetically. 'Do you want to know what about?'

'Yes.' Then, because her voice had been a little bit desperate, a little bit raw, she repeated herself. 'Yes, please.'

Still there was a tremor in her voice and the cameraman gave her an odd look before continuing. He couldn't understand her fear. And maybe…please…the fear was illogical.

'I heard Robbie say he'd guessed a place where someone

called Hamish might be,' the man told her. 'He wanted to go there but Hubert was saying he had to wait for you. As I came within sight, the kid seemed to lose it. He yelled that he'd waited and waited and he had to go now, because Hamish would be stuck. When Hubert said he couldn't go by himself he said he'd take Elspeth. Would that be the dog?'

'Right.' She bit her lip. Where…?

'Will you go search for Robbie straight away?' The cameraman cast an uneasy glance at Hubert, and Morag shook her head. An appendicectomy meant that both Grady and Jaqui would be fully occupied. She'd have to stay with Hubert until one of them could take over.

But Robbie needed her. He needed her so much.

He'd needed her all day and she'd left him alone.

'Hey, it'll be fine,' the cameraman said gently, and she caught herself and managed a faltering smile. She was scaring him. She was the doctor. She was in charge. So she had to get on with it.

'I… Of course it'll be fine.

'We'll take the old man down to the hospital and then we'll find your kid.'

'Thank you.'

'It makes good copy,' he told her.

'I didn't think you were supposed to be involved in breaking news,' she told him, striving for lightness. 'If you're not careful, you'll be on the front page of your paper as a hero.'

'It's you who's the hero,' he told her. 'And there's not a man, woman or child on this island who'd disagree with me.'

CHAPTER ELEVEN

DOWN at the hospital tent, the cardiograph showed no significant change. No significant damage. Morag read the tracing and breathed a little easier.

Maybe Hubert would be lucky. At ninety-two he could hardly complain that he hadn't had a good innings, but the old man was part of the fabric of this island. If he died...

The island was going to die anyway, she told herself bleakly as she adjusted his intravenous line and wrote up his medication.

Louise was normally a beaming, bright-faced nurse who saw the world through often infuriatingly rose-coloured glasses, but the woman who helped settle Hubert was white-faced and silent.

'They're saying we have to leave the island,' she whispered.

'Hush,' Morag told her, but Hubert had drifted into a drug-induced sleep and seemed unaware of their presence. For a moment Morag was stung by a pang of pure envy. To just close her eyes...

'It'll be OK,' she told the nurse, and Louise hiccuped on a sob.

'No, it won't. My Bill...he set his little goat cheese dairy up from scratch. Do you know not a goat was killed? Not a single one? They're the cleverest creatures. Bill went up to the dairy last night and they were all there. We wanted to expand, and to say we have to leave...'

But Morag had no comfort to give. She had her own anguish, and her own desperate need.

'Louise, have you seen Robbie?'

'Robbie?'

'He had an argument with Hubert. I imagine he'll have come down here to find me.'

'I haven't seen him,' Louise told her. 'I've been on the front desk, so I'd have noticed.'

Damn, where was he? She couldn't leave until she had back-up for Hubert, she thought desperately, and Grady and Jaqui were totally occupied. 'The appendix is messy?'

'It's burst and it's awful,' Louise told her. 'Dr Reece has been working in there for well over an hour.'

So here it was again. The medical imperative. She needed Grady—or Jaqui—but Grady and Jaqui were both totally occupied.

She had to find Robbie, but if Hubert suffered cardiac arrest...

She couldn't leave.

'I need to find Robbie.'

'You said he's coming here...'

'No. I assumed he was here.' Morag was trying hard not to panic. 'If he was coming here, he'd be here now. He said he was going to find Hamish.'

'But Hamish drowned,' Louise said blankly, and Morag winced.

'We don't know that.'

'It's...it's a reasonable assumption. By now.'

'No.' Morag bit her lip. 'It's not a reasonable assumption. Nothing's reasonable.'

Help! She felt like kicking something, she thought desperately. Or weeping. Or yelling in sheer frustration.

Or all three.

Robbie, she thought frantically. Grady. Dear heaven, she needed Grady.

She couldn't have him. He had his life and she had hers.

'Will you sit with Hubert?' she asked Louise, and the nurse searched her face and gave her a swift hug. These first hours after a coronary event were vital and they both knew it. In a normal intensive care unit, there'd be monitors set to a central desk. Here everything had to be done the old way.

'Of course. But you'll stay within call? Oh, Morag, what are we going to do?'

'I don't know,' Morag told her. 'I don't have a clue.'

She couldn't leave. Not until Jaqui or Grady were free to leave the operating theatre could she go out of call of the old man. Even with Louise sitting by his bed, with Hubert in the early stages of coronary trouble, there had to be a doctor right there.

But Robbie... Robbie...

Someone else would have to search.

She'd call Marcus, she thought, but no sooner had she thought it than the man himself walked through the entrance of the tent. Marcus looked grim. But, then, the whole island looked grim.

'Morag.' He must have been looking for her, as his face changed as she emerged from Hubert's canvas cubicle. But it didn't grow lighter. 'Thank God you're here.'

More problems? She wasn't sure she could cope with anything else. She glanced across in the direction of Grady's makeshift theatre. The lights they'd set up were brilliant, oozing through the canvas and telling her that Grady and Jaqui were still a hundred per cent occupied.

She could hear a man's low, gravelly voice giving orders. Grady. If Grady wasn't here, it'd be she who was trying to cope with Mary's appendix, she thought grimly. She should be thankful for that at least.

'What's wrong?' she asked, forcing herself to turn back to Marcus. To the next problem.

Marcus hesitated. 'Maybe it's nothing.'

'Tell me.' She knew he didn't want to. They knew they were both carrying intolerable burdens, and to place more on each other seemed impossible. But if something else dreadful had happened then she had to hear it, and Marcus knew it. The lines round his eyes grew tighter. There were dark shadows underneath them.

'May's just been with me,' he told her. 'She asked if I could set up a radio link so she could contact the Sydney hospital where her family is.'

Of course. That made sense, Morag thought. Peter and Christine and Lucy were May's family. She'd be desperate about them, as they'd be desperate about Hamish. 'Did she get through?'

'Mmm. That's why I came to find you.'

'Christine?' The head injury. Dear God…

'No. Christine's not worse.' Marcus could see where her thoughts were headed and moved fast to reassure her. 'She's fully conscious and she's been given the all-clear. But Lucy's with her parents now. That's why I'm here. You know Lucy wouldn't speak to May?'

'She'd hardly speak to anyone.'

'That's right. But now her mother's made her talk. It seems she thinks she knows where her brother might have gone.'

'She knows where Hamish went?'

'She's guessing. Apparently he's been doing…what he's been doing for a while. Lucy knew she should tell her parents, but she didn't, and then when the wave came she realised he must have been killed and she felt like it was all her fault. And she couldn't tell you either because…well, it's Robbie.'

Robbie. Her heart seemed to stand still.

'What about Robbie?'

'She thought…she assumed they were together.'

'Doing what?'

There were small trickles of terror inching down Morag's spine. There was something about the way Marcus was speaking. It was as if he was giving really, really bad news. He was giving her bad news about Hamish, but where was Robbie?

The vision of Hamish's cheeky face was suddenly before her. Hamish and Robbie. The two little boys treated this island as their own personal adventure playground.

Where…?

'It seems they've been robbing petrel nests,' Marcus told her.

'Petrel nests?' She forced her panic to the backburner. Panic was useless. She had to think. The petrels were big seabirds, twice the size of gulls and many times more fierce. They nested on the far side of the island, on rugged, crumbling cliffs that dropped straight to the western shore. The sea there was a mass of jagged rocks and savage breakers. This was the place where the *Bertha* had gone aground all those years before, with the loss of a hundred and sixty-eight lives. A dreadful place.

'They've been climbing the cliffs?' she whispered, appalled.

'Lucy said Hamish boasted about it one day when she'd called him a baby,' Marcus told her. 'It's a game. One of them climbs up and grabs an egg, then he has to bring it down without smashing it, holding it in his hand to keep it warm. The other has to get it back to its original nest. Then he chooses another egg and it starts again. They push themselves to reach harder and harder places. When he told Lucy what they were doing and she threatened to tell Christine, Hamish said it wasn't really dangerous because there were rocks at the bottom and they could climb around from the beach on the south side. It was only the birds that worried them.'

'Only the birds?' Morag drew in her breath in horror, thinking of the birds with their razor-sharp beaks and fierce claws, attacking the little boys as they defended their young. 'Only the birds? Marcus, they… How…? When…?'

'Apparently they've been telling you and Christine that they've been going to the school playground,' he said ruefully. 'With their skateboards.'

She closed her eyes. A nine-year-old, to be putting himself in this sort of danger. What sort of a guardian was she? What sort of a—?

'Hey, Morag, I did it,' Marcus said ruefully, eyeing her with concern. 'My dad caught me and my brother at it when I was their age and we got what-for. I'd forgotten about it. But apparently they've thought of it again all by themselves. And maybe… If Hamish's alternative was to spend his Sunday afternoon doing homework or practising his new skill by himself—well, I know what I'd have done.'

She looked at him as if he were mad. There was even a hint of admiration in his eyes. He had to be kidding! Admiration at such a time. When a little boy could be stuck… Could be washed off.

One little boy?

Or two?

Where was Robbie? On that awful cliff?

For one awful moment she thought she might faint. The world wavered, but just as she started to sway a man's hand gripped on her shoulder.

Grady. It was Grady, still in his theatre gown. He held her, steadied her and waited for the dizziness to pass.

'What's happening, love?' he asked gently, and she winced. But somehow the feel of him was enough. Somehow she collected herself. Love… What on earth did he think he was doing, calling her *love*?

'Don't call me love,' she whispered, and it was all she could do not to burst into tears. She turned her attention frantically back to Marcus. 'Marcus, surely those cliffs have been searched?'

'Maybe not,' he admitted. 'I mean…hell, Morag, you know how rough they are. Why would we look there? But now… I was just coming to find you. I thought—if you didn't mind—we'd take Robbie out in one of the fishing boats and get him to show us exactly where they climbed.'

'But Robbie's gone,' Morag said blankly. 'He's gone to find Hamish. He ran away from Hubert about an hour ago. Dear God, if he guessed where Hamish might be, he'll have gone to the cliffs.'

'He can't have,' Marcus told her, while Grady watched in concern.

'Why not?' he asked.

'The base of the cliffs, where they'd usually scramble

around…the force of the wave knocked it into the sea,' Marcus told them. 'I've noticed the collapse on our way in and out of the harbour as we've been searching. That's what makes me think, if Hamish was up on those cliffs when the wave struck— if he was high enough to be safe from the wave—there's a possibility that he might not have been able to get back. He might be stuck. It's just a small hope but it's worth a look.'

'Well worth a look,' Grady said firmly. He put his arm around Morag and pulled her hard against him. She couldn't pull away. She'd have fallen over if she had. 'I overheard what Marcus has been saying,' he told her. 'So we have two missing boys—one of whom might be on the cliff face.'

'But Robbie?' She was past thinking coherently. 'If he was trying to reach Hamish…'

'He'd see pretty fast that he couldn't get round from the bottom,' Marcus said.

'He wouldn't try and climb down from the top?' Grady demanded, and his hold on her firmed as she winced in disbelief.

'He'd be a damned fool to try,' Marcus said bleakly.

'But if he thought he knew exactly where his friend might be…'

'I'm taking the boat around now,' Marcus told them. He hesitated, looking at Morag's bleached face in concern. 'The fastest way to look is from the sea. Maybe…maybe I can take you—or Grady—in case.'

'OK.' Grady moved straight to operational mode now. This was what he was trained for, and it showed. 'Marcus, can you send a team of locals overland to check the clifftops, then organise your boat to play floodlights over the cliff face? I'll bring the chopper from overhead. It's hard to search cliff faces from the air, but we can do it. I'll scramble the team now.'

'Not with Hubert…'

Too much was happening too fast, but there was still the medical imperative. Briefly Morag outlined what was happening to Hubert, and Grady's face grew more grim.

'OK,' he conceded. 'Morag, you stay here.'

But that was too much. 'I'm going.'

'But—'

'I'm going!' Enough was enough. Medical imperatives had just been overtaken by the personal. 'If it's Robbie... You must see that I need to.'

Grady searched her face and came to a decision. 'OK. Maybe that's for the best anyway. Jaqui will only be minutes while she's reversing Mary's anaesthetic. Then she can take over Hubert's care. Marcus, you take Morag on the boat—with a decent complement of competent people. With life jackets. I'll check Hubert and hand over to Jaqui as soon as I can. Tell me who I can take in the chopper to direct us.'

'May's outside, waiting,' Marcus told him. 'She's Hamish's grandmother. There's not a lot of people know the island better than May, and she's desperate to help.'

He'll refuse, Morag thought wildly. May was an elderly lady. To take her in the helicopter in the dark on such a mission as this...

But Grady was made of sterner stuff. 'Tell her to be ready in five minutes,' he told them. 'Meanwhile, you two go. We'll be right behind you.'

Then, before Morag could react, before she could begin to guess what he intended, he bent and he kissed her.

Her world stilled. The panic inside her froze. For these few short seconds... Everything else disappeared.

For this was no light kiss of reassurance. This was the kiss of a man who was giving a message to his woman. *His* woman. It lasted for long seconds, communicating information that was as unmistakable as it was real.

I love you. You're mine. I'll be with you in this, my heart.

The words were unspoken yet unmistakable, and for those few seconds, Morag felt herself surrendering to his kiss. Surrendering to her own desperate need. She was taking as well as receiving. Laying a claim of her own.

I need you, now and for always. Stay with me?

There could be no such claim—no such question. This man

was here only as part of a medical team, to save lives and then use his medical knowledge to declare this island unfit for human habitation. The tough decisions would be made and he'd move on to the next crisis. To the next need.

But for now that need was hers. She clung and took her strength here, where it was offered. She melted into him for this one harsh kiss, this kiss that must end…

They knew it.

It tore Morag apart. It seemed in this overwhelming chaos that all she had between her and madness was the touch of Grady's mouth.

He'd stay with her whatever it took, the kiss said, but she knew it wasn't true.

He'd stay with her only until tomorrow.

Reality was all around them. Someone pushed back the canvas divider between Reception and the makeshift operating theatre, and somehow she reacted. She pulled back from Grady's arms and gazed at him with eyes that mirrored his own gravity, his own uncertainty—maybe even his own fears? Competent and tough as he was, maybe Grady had no answers.

Answers…

She needed so many answers. Somewhere out there in the dark was her own little Robbie. Maybe he'd walk in the door at any minute, frightened about his friend but safe. But Morag no longer believed he was making his way to her.

Not now she knew where Hamish might be.

Robbie was dependable—far too dependable for one small boy. But he'd been brought up to be self-sufficient, to make a judgement call when needed. He could decide if a phone call was something he should interrupt his aunt for when she was talking earnestly to someone who was crying on their doorstep. If someone appeared at their back door, bleeding, Robbie would find a towel and tell them to press hard before he ran to find Morag. If Morag wasn't home when he got back from school—if she'd been called away on an emergency and hadn't had time to make provision for him—then he'd take himself off to his Aunt Christine's.

Normal kids—normal nine-year-olds with milk-and-cookie mums—would never be asked to make decisions such as these, but with a doctor-mother and then a doctor-aunt, Robbie had been asked to make them almost from birth.

So now Morag knew instinctively the decision Robbie would have made. He was worried sick about his best friend. Morag hadn't appeared before dark to help him, and he hadn't been able to ask Hubert to go with him.

So he'd gone alone.

Grady was still watching her. His calm eyes were a caress in themselves, and she accepted it because she needed it so much.

She gave him a faltering smile in return.

'Take care of Hubert for me,' she whispered. 'And, Grady, come as soon as you can.' She reached out and touched him, lightly on the hand. It was a fleeting gesture that meant nothing—and everything.

'Thank you, Grady,' she whispered. 'My love…'

CHAPTER TWELVE

IT WAS not a good night to be out of the harbour mouth.

The sea, as flat as a millpond during the chaos of the tidal wave, had started to stir. A building sou'westerly was driving a strong, erratic swell in against the cliffs. As soon as the *Minnow-Eater* emerged from the harbour, the fishing boat started an erratic bucketing.

'You do that life jacket up tight, lass,' Marcus called, and she nodded and hauled the straps tighter as she huddled into her oversized waterproofs.

Marcus's boat was one of the best equipped available. They were very lucky it hadn't been in the harbour when the wave had come, but, then, most of the boats had been out. Thankfully. Otherwise they'd have been destroyed.

Marcus headed a crew of four, usually rostered down to three. The town had been lucky it had been Marcus who had been rostered off the day before, but Morag was grateful he hadn't rostered himself off now. The big fisherman was calmly competent, and in this sea they needed every trace of competence they could get. It was a sea that would have an inexperienced fisherman running for cover.

Marcus and Grady were alike, she thought inconsequentially. The two men were separated in age by twenty years but they were really similar. Grady could be just like this in twenty years. But then...

Grady would never look as Marcus did, she thought bleakly. Marcus loved his wife and his kids and his island. He looked at life through calm eyes, with a placid acceptance and muted pleasure with his chosen lot in life.

Whereas Grady... Grady had been here for less than two days and already he was thinking about moving on.

The boat swung south. The moon was lifting over the horizon—thankfully the sky was clear so they'd have moonlight to search. As they rounded the headland Morag could see the brilliant beam from the lighthouse.

Her lighthouse.

If she moved away from the island, if she wasn't here and something happened—another sea-eagle crashed into the lantern room, anything…

Stop it, she thought fiercely. Stop it.

Robbie…

Robbie. Grady. Her island. Her people.

So much to care about. So much to think about. So much, she felt ill.

They were moving fast. The boat was crashing over the cresting swells. Marcus took the boat wide of the rocks that jutted from the southern tip of the island, and then curved in again. Suddenly the sea seemed calmer, but that was an illusion. It was only because they were moving with the same motion as the swell.

'You feeling OK?' Marcus yelled over the noise of the big diesel engine, and she nodded.

'Fine,' she yelled back. Not seasick at least. Just sick with fear.

'There's the boyfriend.' Marcus jabbed a finger skyward and she saw a faint light lifting off from the ridge. Grady had moved fast. It had been twenty minutes since they'd left and already he had his crew mobilised for take-off.

What had Marcus called him? Her boyfriend?

That was a joke.

'We're going in close now,' Marcus told her, and one of the men came toward her with a clip and harness.

'Lifelines,' he told her. 'We lay craypots in here, but not normally in weather as rough as this. It's safe enough if you know what you're doing—and we know what we're doing—but we put the lifelines on anyway.'

'Fine.'

They were nearing the cliffs. Morag had been out here during the day many times as she and her father and sister had fished the waters. She knew these cliffs. In the daytime they were steep and jagged and alive with a mass of seabirds. Now they were dark and forbidding. The sound of the waves crashing on the jagged rocks all but drowned the sound of the boat's big engine.

Robbie. Hamish. The man who'd clipped her lifeline switched on the floodlights.

Where were they?

Their light swept up and down the cliff face in long searching runs. Over and over. Over and over.

Was this stupid? Morag was straining to see along the rockface. Had Hamish been washed out to sea long before this? Was Robbie even now searching somewhere on the island for a friend he'd never find? Alone—as he'd been alone for too long.

She wouldn't cry. She hadn't cried when she'd left Grady or when Beth had died. She mustn't cry now.

But the thought of Robbie alone… Searching for Hamish as they were now doing, but with no one to hold onto him….

Her eyes were still desperately following the line of the floodlights, but she was becoming more afraid by the minute.

The helicopter had reached the cliff face now. Grady. His machine was hovering above them at the far end of the breeding grounds. The helicopter's floodlights scanned to the cliff face and joined the raking, searching lines of light.

At least if the boys were somewhere here they'd know people were looking, Morag thought desperately. Everyone was looking.

Grady was looking. The thought gave her an indefinable comfort, though how one man could make a difference…

He couldn't. Block out Grady.

Search.

Her eyes were straining upward until they hurt. They were only about fifty yards from the base of the cliffs now, as close

as Marcus dared to go. Between the boat and the cliffs were
rocks, freshly tumbled into the sea as the tsunami had smashed
the cliff face and the ledge at the base of the cliffs had crum-
bled. Above the tumbled rocks in the sea there were jagged
crevices filled with sleepy birds staring outward, indignant as
the floodlight interrupted their sleep.

The floodlights raked on. The rockface curved in, out, in…
Morag was holding the rail, leaning forward, her body swaying
with the movement of the sea. Her father had spent so much
of his time on the sea and she with him. And Beth. Her family.

Robbie…

The boat jerked, bows downward, as a breaker foamed over
the stern and water rushed over the deck. Morag's hold on the
rail tightened but her eyes didn't leave the cliff.

Please…

'We'll have to go further out,' Marcus called, and Morag
half turned toward him.

But as she did so, the man who'd adjusted her lifeline gave
a hoarse shout, filled with disbelieving hope.

'There. Two thirds of the way up. Shift the flood to the right.
No. Hell, I thought I saw—I thought…'

The beam shifted. Shifted some more.

And then Marcus was hauling the wheel round and someone
was lunging for the radio. For there on the ledge…

'It's Hamish.' Morag was staring, as if at any minute the
sight would disappear. But it wasn't imagination. A little boy
waving wildly, screaming, as if they could hear over the sound
of the wind and the waves and the engine.

'It's Hamish.' There were tears suddenly cascading down her
cheeks. Here at last there was one happy ending. Hamish. She
could tell Robbie… He couldn't have found his friend yet, she
thought wildly. Here was Hamish, and the land party would
find Robbie as they searched the clifftops. They'd be able to
tell him…

'The chopper will be able to get him off,' Marcus was calling. 'They'll lower someone by harness.'

Of course. Morag didn't dare to take her eyes from the child—as if in losing sight of him she might lose him for ever—but she was aware that the helicopter had already changed course. Now it was zooming downward with its own lights. Grady was up there, she thought wildly, almost dizzy with relief. She'd be able to ring Christine and Peter with such good news. Grady would come down and swoop the child up and he'd be safe...

'Is that a dog?' Marcus asked, narrowing his eyes against the spray.

Hamish was standing on a ledge, half-hidden by a boulder that must be protecting him from the worst of the elements. He was still yelling and waving, as though he hadn't realised they'd seen him, though it must have been obvious.

'I reckon I can see two dogs,' the man beside her said. He had a pair of field glasses in his hand and he wiped them clean and handed them to Morag. 'Two bloody dogs. Where did they come from? Isn't one that the dopey mutt of William Cray's?'

William's border collie. Of course. The big dog often got bored with William's solitary writing, and he'd been known to take off with the boys on their adventures.

So here was another blessing. Morag lifted the glasses and saw the big black dog slink behind Hamish's legs as if terrified of the noise and light. As well he might be.

'I can only see one dog,' she said. 'I'm sure it's William's. He'll be so pleased.'

But...

Something caught her suddenly. A jarring note amidst the joy.

Morag stared on through the salt-sprayed glasses. Hamish was still yelling. Screaming. He still looked terrified, Morag thought.

But why? Why terrified? Hamish wasn't a kid who'd be afraid of a helicopter. The ledge he was standing on looked wide enough. Solid enough. He'd be hungry and thirsty and cold, but...terrified?

They were coming in to rescue him. Surely he should be starting to be reassured?

She took the glasses from her eyes and wiped the salt mist again. Refocused.

And then she froze. The man beside her had been right. From out behind the boulder came a second dog. A golden retriever.

Dear God.

'It's Elspeth,' she whispered, almost to herself. 'It's Hubert's dog.'

Her mind shifted to overdrive and then moved up another notch. Elspeth was with Robbie. Elspeth had left Hubert's place with Robbie, and Elspeth would only have left Robbie to go back to Hubert.

Hubert was in hospital.

If Elspeth was down on that ledge, she'd have come down with Robbie.

Robbie must have tried to climb down from the top.

Her glasses swung back to the child's face. To the unmistakable terror on Hamish's face. To his frantically waving arms. The little boy was staring out at them, but every other second he was glancing down at the water.

Down…

'Robbie's in the water,' she screamed. She lunged for the floodlight but the men were there before her, hauling the light away from the child on the ledge and down to the blackness and foam around the rocks.

'Where…?'

They saw him together in a wash of water. A flash of carrot hair among the foam. An arm waved in a feeble call for help. Marcus yelled a warning, and so did the man beside her.

Morag didn't yell.

He must have tumbled from above, she thought. The sea right at the base of the cliff was relatively free from rocks, or he'd already be dead. He'd fallen and been washed out to where the remnants of the original ledge formed a vicious circle of jagged rocks, holding him enclosed.

Not that there was anywhere for him to go. If he tried to reach the cliffs, he'd be smashed against the cliff. The surf was surging in through gaps in the rocks between him and the boat. There was no way he could swim out to where the water was clearer.

The floodlight was washing the water now in brilliant white and Morag caught a glimpse of a face…

Of terror.

The next wave slammed into him. Dear God, how long had he been there? He was going under.

'Get me a lifeline,' she screamed. She was unhooking herself from the lines set up round the boat and dragging off her waterproofs, kicking off her shoes as she ran along the deck to the bow of the boat. The closest point.

'Grady will come down,' Marcus yelled. He reached out and grabbed her arm. 'We're in radio contact. He's in a harness.'

'It'll take time. Robbie's going under now. I'm going in.'

'You can't. You'll be smashed on the rocks.'

'Then we'll be smashed together. But I can do this. Clip a line on me now or I'm going in without.'

He was staring at her in horror. 'I'll go.'

'I can swim better than you can, and you know it.' It was a skill she'd gloried in as a kid—trained in a city squad, she'd been able to beat any kid on the island.

Marcus knew it. And he'd seen that tiny face washed by the wave. He knew it'd take minutes to get the lines down from the helicopter—minutes Robbie didn't have.

He wasted no more time. He barked a command for someone to take the wheel, then hauled a line free to clip it to her harness.

'Go,' he muttered.

She'd rid herself of the last of her waterproofs. Now she straightened. She focused one more time on exactly where Robbie was—there was a tiny flash of colour and that was all.

She dived deep into the mess of rocks and surf and the darkness.

*   *   *

Grady had moved fast. As soon as Jaqui was free to take over Hubert's care, he had May and the crew into the helicopter, and the chopper was rising almost before they'd hauled their gear out. _

Kids…

Rescue missions were always fraught, always emotional, but when it was kids it seemed a thousand times worse. 'There might be a kid on the cliffs,' he told the crew, and it took just one look at May's drawn face as he helped her into Jaqui's usual seat for the crew to know how serious the situation was.

And Grady wasn't expecting a happy ending here. After all, what were the odds? That a kid had been caught high enough to escape the wave but still be safe almost a day and a half later?

It didn't stop them moving fast. The boat below had beaten them to the cliff face, but only just. They started the long raking of the cliffs with their searchlight with an intensity that said if the child wasn't found, it wouldn't be for want of trying.

And then the boat's light found Hamish… It was a magic moment. A miracle moment.

May cried out with shock and joy—but it was too much for her to take in. She was so shocked that her stomach reacted.

Doug handed her a sick-bag but she was left to fend for herself as they started to fasten Grady into his harness.

'You reckon you can get in close enough to be safe?' Grady demanded of his pilot, and Max nodded.

'I think so. What I'll do is go above the level of the cliff. We'll lower you from there so if the wind gusts up, we won't get slammed into the rockface.'

'Thanks very much,' Grady told him, knowing it was he who'd hit rock. But that was OK. He knew enough to ward off rock with his boots—hell, he'd practised this manoeuvre a hundred times.

'I guess we could land and lower someone from dry land,' Doug said, and Grady looked out, considering.

'We'll get the dogs off that way in the morning. But the land up there's too rocky to get close and I want the kid up now.'

They all did. The boy looked fine—wonderful, even—standing yelling at the helicopter for all he was worth—but he'd been alone for too long already.

The way he was yelling spoke of hysteria.

'You'll get him,' May whispered from the reaches of her sick-bag, and Grady put a hand on her shoulder and gripped, hard.

'I'll have him with you in minutes. The dogs will have to wait...'

'Dogs?'

But she didn't get further. The radio crackled into life. 'Robbie's in the water,' a man snapped.

What?

The boat's floodlights had suddenly veered downward. Max hauled the chopper outward. 'Get me beams below,' he yelled.

'Who...?' May was almost incoherent.

But Grady wasn't listening. He was lying on his stomach on the chopper floor, staring straight down. A tiny copper-coloured head.

And then...

'She's going in,' Doug yelled.

Grady turned toward the boat.

And Morag was in the water.

Morag surfaced, spluttering for air in the foam. She was being washed against the rocks, and she had to get clear, through the gap to where she'd last seen Robbie.

At least the floodlights let her see, in the tiny fractions of time when the surf receded.

To her left...a gap in the rocks.

She turned and a breaker bore down on her. She duck-dived, then surfaced again.

Now.

With every ounce of strength she possessed, she swam for

the gap. Let her get to mid-gap before the next breaker struck…

It struck and she was washed forward, tumbled into the cauldron of foam.

Somehow she surfaced, hoping desperately she was where she'd aimed to be.

There was no reason in the surge of the water. There was no gap between breakers. The surf was like a giant washing machine—worse, a washing machine with jagged rocks and no bottom to hope to find a footing.

And somewhere here…Robbie?

'Robbie?' She was screaming into the dark and the terror of the unknown. 'Robbie!'

The lights were focusing—from both boat and helicopter. She was suddenly in a flood of brilliant light, but she couldn't see.

'Robbie?'

A wall of water smashed against her, driving her back against the rocks she'd just surged past. She felt her leg buckle and a shard of pain shot through her leg.

She'd thought she'd had room for no more sensation. Wrong.

'Robbie!'

She struck out, forward, into the centre of the cauldron. Away from the rocks.

'Robbie…'

A hand clutched her hair.

She was jerked sideways, but she didn't hesitate. All the times of her childhood, with her father on the beach where they'd practised surf lifesaving drill, came to the fore. When grabbed, grab back. Hard. Under the arm, lift, break, turn. Face the victim away from you, and move with force. You're no help to anyone if you drown.

Over and over her father had practised the manoeuvre with both Beth and Morag. Even aged seven or eight, she could break away from a grown man.

So now the hand gripping her head was struck upward but seized at the same time. Robbie? It had to be Robbie.

She hauled him round so he was facing away from her. And, gloriously, she felt him respond to her hold. She felt him curve into her.

Then, for the first time, she could accept that she'd found him.

'It's Morag,' she screamed. 'Don't fight me. Robbie, don't fight.'

He didn't. The hand that had reached for her must have contained the last ounce of strength he possessed.

He slumped.

She clung on.

Another wave smashed her forward. Her right leg wouldn't work—wouldn't move. The pain… She was treading water with one leg—that was all she could do. Her lifejacket was holding her up, sort of, but the tumult of water was making it almost impossible to breathe.

She still had a line holding her, and the line was attached to the boat, but a lot of use that was. If they tried to drag her back through the gap…

They couldn't. They'd know it.

She had to stay out of the range of the rocks.

Another wave jarred her forward. A submerged rock struck her leg, and she heard herself crying out again.

In her arms Robbie stirred and whimpered.

He was still OK, she thought. He was still alive. All she had to do was hold on.

Grady would come.

Please…

'Two lines.' Grady was out on the skids already. 'Just hand me two lines.'

'I'll come in with you.' Doug was clipping a harness in place at Grady's front so all he had to do was find someone, pull them into the harness and be dragged back up. Simple…

'Yeah, and who'll operate the line?' Grady was feeling sick. Of all the times for them to be flying without their full complement… All Max's attention had to be on the helicopter, maintaining its hover, and he needed Ron on the spotlight. Elsey had gone with Hazel to make sure she was settled in William's cottage—and also to surreptitiously check on William—and there'd been no time to wait.

Usually, if there were two in the water they'd both go in. But that was in open seas. Two people in that maelstrom below them would be no use at all. It'd only add to the confusion and double the risk.

Doug knew it. He held Grady by the shoulder for a fraction of a moment and gripped, hard.

'Go.'

Her leg was dragging her down.

How could a leg drag her down? She was wearing a life jacket. She had Robbie securely under his arms, clutched against her breast. If only the water would stop smashing her…

If only her leg would stop dragging…

'Morag!'

The yell seemed to come from a long way away, but in this white water even a foot was vast distance.

But she'd heard him through her fog of pain and fear. Grady was coming. She knew he was coming.

There was a knife in her thigh.

'Morag…' She felt a sharp jerk sideways. And then another. He was coming. He must.

Once Grady had touched the water there was no chance of finding them by sight. He'd been lucky when he'd been lowered to find a line right under him. He guessed what it was straight away—the line linking Morag to the boat—and he sent a silent blessing to whatever fates might be helping him.

Help him some more.

She had to be at the end of the line. Just pray the line didn't catch on a rock and snap.

Just pray.

Hand over hand…

Morag.

She was here! His hand reached out and touched her, and she was his! He reeled her in and held her tight as the next surge of water threatened to carry her away from him. He was clipping himself to her, clipping himself to the harness she thankfully already wore, but his hands still held her. The power of these waves could rip them apart at any minute.

'I'm here,' he told her, pulling her strongly into him. As he did he felt what she held.

She had the boy.

The three of them were linked.

'Morag…'

'Take him,' she managed. She twisted around so that Robbie was between them, so he could slip his spare blue and orange harness around the little boy's midriff and click the metal links into place. Then, with the attachment complete, she gave him a shove that should have sent him away from her.

It didn't.

'Take him. Please… Lift him out of here.' She was screaming but he could barely hear her.

The child seemed unconscious. Normally he'd be turning him, seeing if he was breathing, trying to give a few short breaths. But to try and assess him here was impossible.

To stay longer was risking all their lives.

'I'll be all right,' Morag was screaming. 'Go.'

He'd attached the spare line to her. It wasn't a lift harness— he couldn't take her up without breaking her arms. He'd have to be lowered again to retrieve her.

But to let her go…

There was no choice. Move, Reece, he told himself. The sooner you get him up, the sooner you can come back for her.

Morag.

He caught her with the arm that wasn't holding Robbie and somehow, crazily, he managed to kiss her. Kiss? Sort of a kiss. Certainly not the best kiss he'd ever given a woman. But maybe it was the most important. His lips just managed to brush her face, and then with a wrench that cut like a knife he let her push him away.

He gathered the child tighter against him. Then he raised his arm in the air. Above their heads Doug saw the signal for Max to lift.

They wouldn't waste time trying to winch Grady and Robbie into the helicopter. They'd land him on the clifftop, Grady thought as he swung upward, over the mass of surging water. May could help then. May must help. If the clifftop searchers weren't there yet, then they'd put May out to care for the child while he returned for Morag.

Unless Robbie needed resuscitating, he thought desperately. Why wasn't the child stirring? If there was a medical imperative for him to stay…

Jaqui wasn't with them.

Dear God, no.

Please…

Morag waited.

The pain in her leg had taken her so far to the edge that she had no strength left to fight the water. Somehow she managed to breathe. Somehow she managed to struggle enough to gasp for breath as the life jacket stopped her sinking.

Robbie was gone.

Grady was gone.

They were safe?

A wave slapped her face. Another. She choked and choked again, and struggled to turn away from the wash of water. The pain jabbed through her leg with an intensity she hadn't believed possible.

Grady…

Help me.

She didn't know whether she said it. She had no way of telling. What was reality and what was nightmare? Who could say?

Grady...

The water smashed her against the rock again. Her leg... Robbie...

Grady.

It was too much. She'd done all she could do and more.

She let herself slip away into the dark.

CHAPTER THIRTEEN

SHE was lying in the sun.

Morag let her eyes open—just a little—and the rays of the early morning sun were playing over her face.

Heaven?

It was unbelievable but for the moment she asked no questions. She was warm and dry and there was sunlight.

Robbie.

The thought jarred her eyes wide. The light hurt and she closed them again, but as she did so, a strong hand caught hers. And held.

'Morag.'

It was Grady. Grady was holding her.

She risked the sunlight again and there he was, right in front of her.

She was in bed. In a sea of white. White coverlet, white canvas around her...

But Grady was in green. Theatre garb? She gazed up at him, trying to bring him into focus, trying to make him real.

Not a dream. Please...

'Robbie,' she whispered, and her voice didn't seem to belong to her. Her throat hurt.

Her leg. What was wrong with her leg? It seemed heavy. Unbearably heavy.

'Robbie,' she croaked again, and then Grady was gathering her into his arms, tenderly so as not to disturb the mass of lines that seemed to be attached to her at every angle.

'Robbie's fine,' he said, and his voice didn't seem normal either. 'He's asleep. Look.' He moved her gently so she could see across to the next bed. Robbie's hair was a splash of colour against his pillows, and his freckles stood out on his too-pale

174

face. 'He was awake in the night, asking for you,' he told her. 'But he was content to wait until you woke.'

'In the night?' She stared wonderingly out into the sunlight.

She was in the field hospital. She and Robbie seemed to have a 'room' to themselves.

Someone—Grady?—had lifted a flap of canvas, hooking it high so she could see the sun rising over the horizon.

Dawn...

'I've been asleep?'

'For long enough.' He held her as he'd hold a piece of Dresden china—as if she might crack at any minute. 'We operated on your leg last night. Compound fracture. Hell, Morag, you might have lost your leg.'

She let that sink in. It was like a story about someone else. 'So you and Jaqui operated—as you operated on Sam.'

'Not quite like Sam,' he told her, and his hold on her tightened. 'Your leg's going to be OK. We would have sent you to Sydney but the blood supply was compromised. You'll need another operation before you're through, but for now...for now you're safe.'

That was enough for the moment. He held her in silence while she absorbed what she'd been told.

Safe...

They were good words, she thought dreamily. 'You're safe.' She wasn't dead. She wasn't in heaven. She was alive, in Grady's arms.

And Robbie? She still had questions.

'You're sure Robbie's OK?' Her voice still seemed to be coming from a long way away.

'He ate eggs and bacon at midnight. He's suffered a couple of nasty lacerations and some bruising, and he's had a huge fright, but as soon as he realised you and Hamish were OK, the whole thing started fading to an adventure.'

Good. That was good.

Why wouldn't her sluggish mind think?

'Hamish?' she managed.

'He ate eggs and bacon at midnight, toasted sandwiches at five and I think he's complaining that he's hungry again now. He was a little dehydrated, but he drank so much lemonade after we dragged him up that we didn't bother putting a drip up.'

'Oh, Grady...'

'And the dogs are fine, too,' he told her in a voice that was decidedly shaky. 'The team decided they wouldn't leave them there overnight, so Doug and Max lowered themselves over the cliff face and brought them up in harnesses. Doug took Mutt home, and William's decided he's going to wait a bit before he starts the antidepressants. The first couple of days' medication can bring drowsiness, and William has too much to do to be drowsy.'

Then, at the look of sheer confusion on her face, he smiled down at her with a gentleness that turned her heart right over. 'That's all,' he told her. 'You're barely with me, my heart. But you are with me. That's all that matters. For now...you need to sleep.'

Sleep.

It seemed a good option to her. Even a great option. Her eyes were so tired.

But still she clung, and still he held. She could feel the beating of his heart, she thought dreamily. Her Grady...

Her heart was beating with his. What more could she ask?

Nothing.

She woke again and Grady wasn't there. Robbie was gone from the next bed, but Louise was watching. The nurse fussed and clucked and went and heated some soup. She helped Morag drink a little then she adjusted her pillows, checked her drip and told her not to worry.

'Robbie's with Hamish. He's fine. Can you believe that child? He's scratched to pieces and an adult would be groaning for days, but William's brought Hamish down.'

She looked confused. Why wouldn't she look confused?

'William's brought Hamish down?'

'Hamish and May are staying with William because of the dogs, and also because Hazel was so pleased. You know Hazel and May are cousins? After losing Elias, finding Hamish has cheered Hazel up like nothing else could. It's cheered everyone up. Now the two boys and the dogs are sitting out in the sun, comparing adventures.'

Adventures... There'd been too many adventures. 'They won't go back onto the cliff?'

'Are you kidding? I don't think they ever want to see that cliff again in their lives. William's told them if they wander from sight he'll scalp the pair of them, and they've promised. You know they're kids who keep their promises.'

They were, too. But...

'Grady.' She was thinking aloud. 'Where's Grady?'

'He's at the town meeting. Like everyone else except Irene and me—we're keeping the hospital running.' She gave a tight, distracted smile, and her pleasure in talking of the little boys faded a little. 'Which is just as well. Someone has to.'

'The meeting.' Morag's mind focused sharply. 'Oh, no, the meeting... Louise, I need to be there.'

'Right, so you can just pick up your bed and leave? I don't think so.' The nurse smiled and started to fit a blood-pressure cuff. 'Stop your worrying, girl,' she told her. 'You've been doing too much worrying. About everyone. And now Grady's worrying about you, and William's worrying about you, and Marcus and May and Hazel and just about everyone else on the island.'

'But—'

'You know you've got a really nasty fracture of your leg?' Louise sounded as if she was scolding. 'Jaqui and Grady worked like fury to try and re-establish a blood supply, and you're dead lucky your leg didn't to go the way of Sam's. So if you think you can just get up and keep going, you're gravely mistaken.'

'I must,' she said in distress. 'The island… If I'm out of action they'll evacuate the island and we'll never return.'

Louise's kindly face clouded. 'I don't know about that,' she said stolidly. 'But there's nothing you and I can do about it, and worrying won't help. So how about I call Irene to double-check the drugs, and we'll give you the injection Dr Reece ordered? That'll stop the pain and let you settle back to sleep. I'd imagine when you wake up, everything will be decided.'

'Everything will be over.'

Louise pursed her lips and turned to call Irene. 'Wait and see.'

Morag did sleep. Her body gave her no choice. She drifted in and out of a drug-induced stupor all through that long afternoon.

When she woke, the flap of the tent was closed. She could no longer see the sea, and the light was starting to fade.

She winced and groaned a little as the pain in her leg caught. But that wasn't what was worrying her. The effects of the morphine had receded, her mind was clear and she was faced with the overwhelming realisation that she'd missed the meeting.

And she was injured. She understood enough of the injury to her leg to know she'd be off work for many weeks. The island would have no medical officer, and that'd be the death knell to the island. The decision about the island's future was a foregone conclusion.

'It's about time you woke up.'

She twisted and Grady was at the entrance to her makeshift ward.

'Hi, Morag,' he told her, and he was smiling. What a smile. It was a smile to make her catch her breath. 'We've been waiting for you to wake up for ages. Welcome to your future.'

Her future. What on earth was he talking about? She tried hard to focus, tried to see…

We've been waiting for you to wake up?

Who?

Robbie.

Robbie was beside him, clutching his hand as if he belonged there. Robbie and Grady. The two men in her life. Her love for them both was so intertwined, the fact that they stood hand in hand hardly took any explaining. It felt…right.

But Robbie was looking desperately anxious. He mustn't be anxious.

'Robbie,' she whispered, and the little redhead darted toward her like an arrow to its target. She gathered her to him with her free arm and she held him close.

But over his head she looked at Grady.

'What…? What…?'

But there was more to understand. *We*, Grady had said, and he'd meant *we*. It wasn't just Grady and Robbie. There were people behind Grady.

Lots of people.

And they were all smiling.

'Your island's safe,' Grady told her.

'Safe?'

Grady opened his mouth to continue, but he was interrupted.

'We've got a plan.' Jaqui was pushing her way past Grady, elbowing him aside as if he were an annoying obstacle. She was dressed in her yellow overalls—so was Grady. And there was Doug in his overalls and…more…

'Grady wanted to tell you by himself,' Jaqui was saying, 'but I said no way. He said you're not ready for any more than one visitor at a time, but what would he know? He's too close to be your treating physician, so I've elected myself. And joy's not going to kill you, girl. Now, is it?'

'Joy?'

'The meeting,' she said in some satisfaction. 'We knew you'd want to be there. But we couldn't wait. It was far too soon for anyone to be level-headed. Only two days after something as massive as a tsunami, there's been so little time to think. But decisions had to be made immediately. Either everyone needs to work like crazy and get some sort of drainage and water system in place, or we all get out of here now. The infrastructure's so damaged there's a real health risk.'

'She knows that. Don't waffle,' Grady said darkly, trying to edge her aside again, but Jaqui refused to be edged.

'Who's waffling? Who had the best idea?'

'Grady did.' It was Marcus, pushing in past Jaqui. The burly fisherman was in front now, and likely to stay that way. After all, he was the biggest. 'It seems Grady's brother's a politician in Sydney, with more clout than we know what to do with. So he's pulled strings like you wouldn't believe.'

'But it's my husband who clinched it,' Jaqui retorted. 'My Craig is the head of a big public works department on the mainland and he's bored. We're both bored. And we have four adult sons living with us who are driving us crazy. Craig's been talking of retirement, but who wants to retire and do nothing? Anyway, we've been thinking about getting away—doing something completely different—and now I've met the island goats...'

'What are you talking about?' It was as much as Morag could do to whisper, and Robbie pulled away from her to stare into her face in concern. Like he was worried she might have bumped her head.

Like she was being adult-obtuse.

'It's easy,' the little boy told her. 'Hubert explained it to me and Grady told me again. Dr Jaqui's husband is an engineer and he's going to come over and start digging drains so we can stay on the island. And Dr Jaqui wants to help with the goats.'

'Craig doesn't exactly dig,' Jaqui conceded. 'But he's really good at organising. And Robbie's right about the goats. Anyway, with Grady's politician brother pulling strings to keep the army lads over here to help, and William's friends moving mountains...'

'William's friends?' Maybe Robbie was right. Maybe she had been hit on her head. Her head was certainly spinning.

William was there, too, she saw, stunned. He was standing at the back, grinning like he'd won the lottery.

'William has the arts community in the palm of his hand,' Grady told her. He was one of ten or so people crowding around her bed now, but suddenly they may as well have been alone. He was smiling and smiling at her, his eyes locked on hers. Promising the world.

But still talking practicalities.

'From the time William got Mutt back, he's been on the end of a phone, contacting every land council—every human rights group—every arts board—to the end that if we take anything away from the Koori people that's been given to them already—like twenty-four-hour medical support—there'll be a national uproar.' Grady turned to smile at William—who was blushing, for heaven's sake. 'It seems the Koori artwork here is known worldwide, and that's given us even more leverage. The elders worked with William on this, Morag, and Yndilla and Nargal even consented to use our radio to confirm their needs with the mainland Koori organisations. You've gained the Koori people's trust, Morag. They want you.'

'But…' She was too dazed to take it in but it wasn't making sense. 'They can't… I have to leave…'

'That's the best bit.' It was Hubert, piping up from the other side of the canvas, and Morag's flimsy side wall was twitched aside to reveal the old man lying in the next cubicle. Like Morag, he was attached to IV lines, but his colour had returned and his voice had a strength that said he might well be good for a few years yet. 'Tell her the best. Tell her.'

'I'm trying to,' Grady said, half laughing.

'He's trying to tell you we're staying,' Jaqui told her. 'Craig and I are staying. I just looked at this place and I knew…'

'You and Craig are staying?'

'I told you,' Jaqui said with exaggerated patience. 'I've fallen for the goats. One licked me on the face when I was trying to sleep in the sun and I was hooked. Craig will oversee rebuilding and I'll be a medical partner. With goats on the side.'

'Me, too,' Grady told her, and the whole world seemed to hold its breath.

'You…you, too?'

'You haven't asked her,' Jaqui told him. 'Bill and Louise can't share their goats with everyone—and Morag might not want a medical partner.'

'That cuts you out, then,' he retorted.

'Well…'

'Jaqui, shut up.'

'Only if you tell her, stupid.'

'Jaqui and I have been talking,' he said a little bit desperately, and she gazed up at him in disbelief.

She was still cuddling Robbie. The little boy was curled against her, but he was gazing up at the crowd around his aunt's bed as if this were a theatre spectacular. And he had the best seat in the house.

'You and Jaqui have been talking?' Morag prodded, and Grady cast a despairing glance around at his audience.

'I don't suppose there's any chance you lot will go away,' he said, and got unanimous grins.

'Not a snowball's chance in a bushfire,' Marcus said calmly. 'Tell her.'

'OK.' He took a deep breath, obviously a man caught between a rock and a hard place. 'Um…I thought I might stay here, too,' he told her.

She thought about it. Her leg should be hurting, she thought dazedly, but she couldn't feel her leg. She couldn't feel anything. Was she floating?

Who needed morphine when this was happening?

But… 'What on earth would you do here? she managed.

'I wouldn't mind a bit of privacy,' Grady tried again.

'It's not going to happen,' Jaqui told him. 'Tell the lady.'

'Yeah, well, Jaqui and I have been talking. And we think—'

'We think this makes a really fantastic base for Air-Sea

Rescue, from here to New Zealand,' Jaqui said. 'There's so much sea traffic…'

'You have to be kidding,' Morag whispered. 'You're crazy.'

'We are a bit,' Grady admitted. 'But we have the government interested in setting up a medical base to service all the remote islands north and east of here. Individually each has tiny populations but when you put them together—'

'It makes economic sense to service them from here rather than send everyone to the mainland.' Jaqui's voice was triumphant.

'And when you add the indigenous populations…' Grady managed.

'The education needs,' William added. 'Health education for the Kooris has to be a priority.'

'Then there's the fact that the lighthouse needs protecting from marauding sea eagles,' Marcus added. 'So we need you and Jaqui and Grady. Plus, I'm going to teach Grady to fish.'

'Me, too,' said Jaqui.

'I can fish already,' Robbie told her. 'I'll help teach you.'

'But—'

'And we're going to run remote training sessions,' Grady added with a flourish, as if it was his trump card. 'Jaqui and William and Marcus and I started work at dawn, planning this. After Jaqui and I sorted your leg out we were too high to sleep, and no one else was sleeping either. There's such potential. We have everything here. We have such expertise.'

'We're the best,' Jaqui said modestly, and everyone laughed.

And then the laughter died.

They were all looking at her, Morag realised. They were all waiting for her reaction.

She couldn't react. She didn't know how to. There was so much to take in…

'The island must remain viable for everyone,' Grady said softly. 'And it can. You know, Angie Salmon stood up at the public meeting today and told everyone that Orlando would be buried here because this was where he belonged. It was where everyone belonged. She said she was staying here and so were her family, and if they took the doctor away then the world would be inflicting another disaster on the island as big as the tidal wave. The cameraman who helped Hubert has resurrected a damaged photograph of Orlando, and the world's press is splashing his picture all over the world's newspapers right now. We're safe, Morag. We're all safe. We're home.'

'You're home? You?' She could hardly take it in.

'I will need to go to Sydney from time to time,' Grady told her, as if he needed to lay all his cards out on the table right now. 'So will Jaqui. We'll still be part of the emergency services network, which is run from the mainland. But we thought—'

'We thought we could go, too.' Robbie was almost gleeful. 'Grady talked about it to me like I was a grown-up. He said you really liked shopping and he bet me that I'd like it, too. He said Sydney has cool stuff. And he said that when I go to school in Sydney, you guys could all come over a lot to visit me. He said you'll have three doctors on the island, so you'll all be able to take turns.'

'You have it all worked out.'

'Yup,' said Grady. 'And this way I get to be assistant light-house-keeper. How cool is that?'

'You've already talked Robbie into it.'

'Yup,' said Jaqui. 'And I'm going to be assistant to the assistant of the lighthouse-keeper.'

'Is there anything you haven't planned?'

'The wedding,' Grady said, and the whole world stilled.

'The…'

'Right.' Enough was enough. Grady squared his shoulders. He turned to face the assembled congregation.

'I'm doing this by myself,' he decreed.

'Hey, don't mind us,' Hubert said.

'You can't keep all the good bits for yourself,' Jaqui added.

'Out,' said Grady. He plucked Robbie from Morag's arms

THE CHILDREN'S HEART SURGEON
by Meredith Webber (Jimmie's Children's Unit)

Paediatric heart surgeon Alex Attwood gives all his caring to his tiny patients. He's not interested in women…not since he kissed a blonde stranger long ago and never found her again! So Alex is shocked to meet new nurse manager Annie Talbot. She may have a different name to his mystery woman – but her response to his kiss is the same!

THE DOCTOR'S LATIN LOVER *by Olivia Gates*
(24/7)

When Dr Javier Sandoval Noriega last saw Savannah Richardson he asked her to marry him – and she laughed in his face. So what is the pampered socialite doing in Colombia as part of Javier's Mobile Surgery Unit? Javier can hardly believe it, but he knows he must get rid of her fast – before he falls in love all over again!

NURSE ON ASSIGNMENT *by Rebecca Lang*

World Aid nurse Lilly Page has gone to Northern Ontario to provide medical aid in the midst of raging forest fires – and to escape her heartache. But it follows her – in the shape of surgeon Rafe Neilson. With danger all around, and emotions running high, can Lilly find the strength to fight her fears and rescue their relationship?

On sale 6th May 2005

MILLS & BOON

Modern romance™ EXtra

Extra passion for your money!

With top selling authors **Miranda Lee**
and **Cathy Williams.**

MIRANDA LEE'S

Secrets & Sins...Revealed!

Intense, Sexy,
Dark Desires
& Dangerous
Secrets

In June look out for Mills & Boon Medical Extra, a
longer novel, Their Baby Miracle from Lilian Darcy!

Available at most branches of WHSmith, Tesco, ASDA, Martins, Borders,
Eason, Sainsbury's and all good paperback bookshops.

www.silhouette.co.uk

0405/154

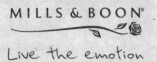

4 FREE

BOOKS AND A SURPRISE GIFT!

We would like to take this opportunity to thank you for reading this Mills & Boon® book by offering you the chance to take FOUR more specially selected titles from the Medical Romance™ series absolutely FREE! We're also making this offer to introduce you to the benefits of the Reader Service™—

- ★ **FREE home delivery**
- ★ **FREE gifts and competitions**
- ★ **FREE monthly Newsletter**
- ★ **Exclusive Reader Service offers**
- ★ **Books available before they're in the shops**

Accepting these FREE books and gift places you under no obligation to buy, you may cancel at any time, even after receiving your free shipment. Simply complete your details below and return the entire page to the address below. You don't even need a stamp!

YES! Please send me 4 free Medical Romance books and a surprise gift. I understand that unless you hear from me, I will receive 6 superb new titles every month for just £2.75 each, postage and packing free. I am under no obligation to purchase any books and may cancel my subscription at any time. The free books and gift will be mine to keep in any case.

M5ZED

Ms/Mrs/Miss/Mr .... Initials ....

Surname .... BLOCK CAPITALS PLEASE

Address ....

....

.... Postcode ....

Send this whole page to:
UK: FREEPOST CN81, Croydon, CR9 3WZ